HELLCAT

Agatha Jennings' message was short but not sweet when she said what Skye could do with the two men he had saved her from.

"Don't be bashful on my account," the buxom redhead told the Trailsman. "If you're inclined to rub these two out, have at it."

"Bitch," one of them snapped.

Fargo had only to shift his weight and lash out with his left boot to connect, his foot smashing into the man where it would do the most damage. The sidewinder doubled over and clutched his groin, his face becoming beet red as he sputtered, gasped, and tottered. Fargo took a step rearward, being careful to hold his knife poised to slash should the other hard case get any fancy ideas. Then, his body a blur, he planted a kick squarely on the first one's jaw. The man dropped like a poled ox.

"Kick him again!" Agatha urged.

Skye Fargo had hooked onto a hellcat with claws—and with as big a lust for bloodletting as hard loving. . . .

⊘ SIGNET (0451)

UNTAMED ACTION ON THE WESTERN FRONTIER

☐ **OUTLAW by Warren Kiefer.** Lee Garland. Since the last Apache uprising made him an orphan child, he's seen it all, done it all, in war, in peace, in the West and East. He's the last great hero in a roaring, rollicking saga that shows how wonderful America is. (169549—$5.99)

☐ **A LAND REMEMBERED by Patrick D. Smith.** Tobias MacIvey started with a gun, a whip, a horse and a dream of taming a wilderness that gave no quarter to the weak. He was the first of an unforgettable family who rose to fortune from the blazing guns of the Civil War, to the glitter and greed of the Florida Gold Coast today. (158970—$5.99)

Prices slightly higher in Canada

Buy them at your local bookstore or use this convenient coupon for ordering.

NEW AMERICAN LIBRARY
P.O. Box 999 – Dept. #17109
Bergenfield, New Jersey 07621

Please send me the books I have checked above.
I am enclosing $_____ (please add $2.00 to cover postage and handling). Send check or money order (no cash or C.O.D.'s) or charge by Mastercard or VISA (with a $15.00 minimum). Prices and numbers are subject to change without notice.

Card #_____ Exp. Date _____
Signature_____
Name_____
Address_____
City _____ State _____ Zip Code _____

For faster service when ordering by credit card call **1-800-253-6476**

Allow a minimum of 4-6 weeks for delivery. This offer is subject to change without notice.

THE TRAILSMAN
135

MONTANA MAYHEM

by

Jon Sharpe

A SIGNET BOOK

SIGNET
Published by the Penguin Group
Penguin Books USA Inc., 375 Hudson Street,
New York, New York 10014, U.S.A.
Penguin Books Ltd, 27 Wrights Lane,
London W8 5TZ, England
Penguin Books Australia Ltd, Ringwood,
Victoria, Australia
Penguin Books Canada Ltd, 10 Alcorn Avenue,
Toronto, Ontario, Canada M4V 3B2
Penguin Books (N.Z.) Ltd, 182-190 Wairau Road,
Auckland 10, New Zealand

Penguin Books Ltd, Registered Offices:
Harmondsworth, Middlesex, England

First published by Signet, an imprint of New American Library,
a division of Penguin Books USA Inc.

First Printing, March, 1993
10 9 8 7 6 5 4 3 2 1

Copyright © Jon Sharpe, 1993
All rights reserved

The first chapter of this book previously appeared in *Cougar Dawn*, the one hundred and thirty-fourth volume in this series.

REGISTERED TRADEMARK—MARCA REGISTRADA

Printed in the United States of America

Without limiting the rights under copyright reserved above, no part of this publication may be reproduced, stored in or introduced into a retrieval system, or transmitted, in any form, or by any means (electronic, mechanical, photocopying, recording, or otherwise), without the prior written permission of both the copyright owner and the above publisher of this book.

BOOKS ARE AVAILABLE AT QUANTITY DISCOUNTS WHEN USED TO PROMOTE PRODUCTS OR SERVICES. FOR INFORMATION PLEASE WRITE TO PREMIUM MARKETING DIVISION, PENGUIN BOOKS USA INC., 375 HUDSON STREET, NEW YORK, NEW YORK 10014.

If you purchased this book without a cover you should be aware that this book is stolen property. It was reported as "unsold and destroyed" to the publisher and neither the author nor the publisher has received any payment for this "stripped book."

The Trailsman

Beginnings . . . they bend the tree and they mark the man. Skye Fargo was born when he was eighteen. Terror was his midwife, vengeance his first cry. Killing spawned Skye Fargo, ruthless, cold-blooded murder. Out of the acrid smoke of gunpowder still hanging in the air, he rose, cried out a promise never forgotten.

The Trailsman they began to call him all across the West: searcher, scout, hunter, the man who could see where others only looked, his skills for hire but not his soul, the man who lived each day to the fullest, yet trailed each tomorrow. Skye Fargo, the Trailsman, the seeker who could take the wildness of a land and the wanting of a woman and make them his own.

Spring, 1859—the Swan Range of the Rockies, where unwary whites often fell prey to bloodthirsty Blackfeet, savage beasts, or their own brutal lust . . .

1

Skye Fargo frowned when he heard the shot.

A big man who moved with the fluid ease of a prowling mountain lion, he paused in a stand of pines on the west slope of a jagged peak and cocked his head to listen for a second report. The shot had come from below and to the north, perhaps a quarter of a mile off. It meant there were others in the area, and because he was in a remote region seldom penetrated by whites, those others must be Indians.

He glanced down at the fresh elk tracks he had been following, his frown deepening. His hope of a succulent steak for supper was now shattered. If he fired his Sharps, he risked having the shot heard by the Indians. And the last thing he wanted was to tangle with a war party of Bannocks or Blackfeet.

Annoyed, he pivoted and headed down the slope. It would be best to pack up, saddle the Ovaro, and get the hell out of there before the Indians stumbled on his camp. He would ride farther west, being careful to skirt Flathead Lake, and enter territory where even the neighboring tribes rarely ventured.

All Fargo wanted was to be left alone so he could hunt, fish, and trap in peace for two or three weeks. In recent months he had spent more time than was his custom in various towns and cities scattered from the Mississippi River to the Pacific Ocean, and he was tired of being among large crowds of people. A loner at heart, he had had his fill of civilization for a while.

The old, familiar longing for the wilderness had returned on a visit to Denver, a longing for the wide open spaces he called his home, where a man could live as he pleased without interference from another living soul. So he had bought extra supplies and ridden north until he reached Fort Benton. From there, he had traveled westward into an isolated range of the majestic Rockies where he wouldn't encounter anyone else.

Or so he had thought.

He'd known, of course, that the Blackfeet, Assiniboin, Atsina, and Crows lived on the plains to the east, and that the Bannocks, Kalispels, Shoshonis, and others all frequented the territory to the west and south. But the range he'd selected was so far off the beaten path, even for the Indians, that he'd figured on enjoying several weeks of uninterrupted solitude.

Sighing in frustration, Fargo hurried, his muscles rippling with latent power. His camp lay half a mile distant, and he feared the Indians might discover it before he got there. Losing his gear was of no consequence, but he couldn't abide the thought of losing his reliable pinto stallion. That horse had saved his hide more times than he cared to count, had carried him across blistering deserts and frigid prairies covered by deep snow, and had taken him from one end of the country to the other and never once given him cause to complain. In a sense, the Ovaro was more like a friend than a dumb beast of burden, and he wasn't about to let it be stolen.

Suddenly more shots split the crisp mountain air, arising from the same direction. There were two quick blasts, followed by a half dozen slightly fainter reports.

Fargo paused again. Those first two had been rifle shots, the others all made by pistols—which might mean there were white men involved since Indians rarely used revolvers. But what would a party of whites be doing in the area? The fur trade had long since died out, and except for a few grizzled diehards who trapped ranges much farther west where beaver were still abundant, the Rockies had seen their last of the wild and woolly trapping fraternity. Prospectors generally confined their activities far to the south near Denver, where gold had recently been discovered, and the nearest settlement was Fort Benton, over one hundred and thirty miles to the east. There was simply no reason for any white man to enter the region Skye was in, which was one of the reasons he had picked it.

Four more pistol shots rang out.

Fargo firmed his grip on the heavy Sharps and broke into a dogtrot. As tirelessly as an Apache, he covered almost the entire half mile when a hint of movement and a glimmer of bright color off to his right drew him up short behind the trunk of a spruce. Automatically he crouched and cocked the rifle, seeking the source of the movement. He saw her right away.

A redhead burst from cover at the opposite end of a meadow bordering the trees. Her hair flying, her features a study in determination, she pumped her limbs furiously, her yellow dress swirling about her shapely legs, her ample bosom heaving from her exertion. Twenty yards she went before she cast a hasty glance over her left shoulder, stumbled in a rut, and fell to one knee.

Fargo was about to step into the open to go to her aid when two men appeared. They were messy-looking characters in shabby clothes. Both held pistols, and both were smirking as they closed in on their redheaded quarry.

The woman cried out, heaved upright, and resumed running for her life.

"Stop, missy!" bellowed the taller of the duo.

Ignoring him, the redhead raced like a frightened fawn toward the shelter of the forest.

"Stop, damn you!" the man barked and snapped off a shot from the hip. The gun spat lead and smoke, the slug kicking up dirt beside her. "The next one will be in your leg," he warned.

With evident reluctance the woman finally halted. Her shoulders slumping, breathing heavily, she turned. "Why are you doing this?" she called out. "What do you want?"

Neither man answered until they were almost to her; then the tall one laughed and raked his hungry gaze from her luxurious hair to her thighs. "What kind of a stupid question is that, missy? You know damn well what we want."

Fargo couldn't see her face, but he noticed her backbone stiffen and admired her gumption when she spoke.

"Yes, I suppose I do. Anyone who rides with Snake Haddock has to be vermin just like him. Haddock wouldn't know how to treat a decent woman if his life depended on it."

"We'll let you tell him that in person when he shows up later," the tall one responded with a sneer.

"Until then," said his companion, "you'd be wise to keep your pretty mouth shut."

"And what if I don't?" the woman defiantly replied.

Fargo tensed when the man backhanded her across the face. Rage welled up within him. Any man who would beat a defenseless woman deserved to be stomped into the ground. She staggered but kept her footing; then she was seized roughly by the tall hard case and pulled northward. Fargo had seen enough! Rising, he sprinted in pursuit, staying shy of the meadow, staying among the trees where his buckskin-clad frame was least likely to be spotted and where he could keep an eye on the redhead and her captors. They entered a tract of pines without once looking back.

Fargo didn't know what he was getting himself into, but he wasn't about to sit idly by and do nothing while the woman was hauled off against her will. He was tempted to shoot both men. Picking them off with the Sharps would be as easy as pie, but the shots were bound to be heard by any friends the pair might have in the vicinity. So it would be better to deal with them silently.

He probed the grove of trees until he spied the woman's yellow dress, then poured on the speed until he was well ahead of the threesome. Slanting to a point directly in their path, he sought cover behind a fir tree, leaned the Sharps against the trunk, and slipped his right hand inside his boot to clasp his Arkansas toothpick. Voices told him the three were slowly approaching.

"—him what he wants to know or he'll have all of you killed," the tall one was saying. "Mark my words, missy. You don't want to get on the bad side of a man like Snake Haddock."

"I didn't know he had any other side," the woman replied sarcastically. "Are you sure we're talking about the same lying, thieving, back-shooting, no-account bastard?"

Fargo heard the tall man sigh. Peeking around the bole, he saw the three of them coming toward him. He guessed they would pass within six feet or so to his left.

"You're asking for grief, Agatha Jennings," the tall one declared. "If you get Snake all riled and he slits your throat, don't say I didn't warn you."

Easing onto his elbows and knees, Fargo scooted to the next tree, using weeds and a bush for cover. Uncoiling, he straightened and waited, scarcely breathing, girding himself for the moment they would come abreast of his hiding place.

"You're all heart, Murdock," the woman declared. "And here Pa told me you're nothing but a low-down skunk."

"Hugh is a fine one to talk. He rode with us for two years, didn't he? He did more than his share of robbing and killing, I can tell you. So where does he get off acting so high and mighty now?"

"He quit. He's trying to reform."

The two hard cases laughed.

"You can't teach an old dog new tricks, missy," Murdock said. "If he told you he was giving up the old ways, he lied."

"Where is it?" the other man asked.

"Where is what?" Agatha responded.

The trio stepped into view, the redhead walking between her captors. Both men were staring at her. Both had returned their revolvers to their holsters.

Fargo launched himself from behind the trunk, reaching the one called Murdock in a single bound and pressing the razor tip of his knife against the tall man's throat before Murdock could react. "Give me any excuse and you're dead," he said, increasing the pressure to emphasize the point.

Murdock had frozen, his eyes wide in surprise.

The other man started to make a move for his six-shooter, then apparently thought better of the notion and stood still, his gun hand poised above his pistol. "Who are you, mister?" he demanded. "What the hell do you want?"

"I want you to pretend you're reaching for a pine cone," Fargo directed, and when the other man hesitated he jabbed the toothpick a bit deeper into Murdock.

"Do as he says, Wolney!" Murdock declared. He gulped and blinked, glancing at Wolney out of the corner of his eye. "If you don't, and if this jasper doesn't kill me, I'll sure as blazes kill you!"

Wolney scowled but complied, extending both arms overhead. "You're making a big mistake, mister," he told Skye. "We ride with Snake Haddock. Give us trouble and you'll answer to him."

So far Agatha Jennings had not spoken a word. She was studying Fargo intently, her brow creased in deep thought, her hands on her slender hips.

"Take three steps straight backward, Miss Jennings," Skye instructed her. "I wouldn't want you to come between Wolney and me. He might get the harebrained idea to go for that Remington on his hip, and then I'd have to kill both these gents."

Smiling ever so sweetly at her frustrated abductors, Agatha Jennings backed up a few feet. "Don't be bashful on my account, stranger." She addressed Fargo. "If you're inclined to rub these two out, have at it."

"Bitch!" Wolney snapped.

Fargo only had to shift his weight and lash out with his left boot to connect, his foot smashing into Wolney where it would do the most damage. Taken unawares, Wolney doubled over and clutched his groin, his face becoming beet red as he sputtered, gasped, and tottered. Fargo took a step rearward, being careful to hold the knife poised to slash should Murdock get any fancy ideas. Then, his body a blur, he planted a kick squarely on Wolney's jaw. The man dropped like a poled ox.

"Kick him again!" Agatha urged.

Ignoring her, Fargo wagged the toothpick in Murdock's face. "How about you? Care to insult the lady?"

"Not me, mister. I know when to play a hand out and I know when to fold."

"Smart hombre," Fargo said and deftly tossed the toothpick from his right hand to his left. In the blink of an eye he drew his Colt, training it on Murdock's chest. The click of the hammer sounded loud in the stillness of the forest. "Now unbuckle your gun belt and let it fall. No tricks or else."

"You don't have to tell me twice," Murdock said, using just one hand to unfasten his belt buckle. As his gun hit the earth he raised his arms, then nodded at the unconscious Wolney. "What are you fixing to do with us?"

"For starters, how about if I teach you some manners?" Fargo said sternly. "First lesson, don't go around hitting folks who can't fight back." With that he hauled off and clubbed Murdock across the face with the Colt barrel. The blow drove the tall man to his knees. Dazed, blood trickling from his nose, Murdock made a sluggish play for his gun. Fargo slugged him again. Down Murdock went, as limp as a wet rag.

Agatha Jennings laughed in delight. "You do know how to handle yourself, don't you, big fella?" she asked, coming forward and looping her arm over Fargo's left elbow.

"I saw them grab you," Fargo said, amused by the twinkle in her lovely green eyes and the frankly suggestive grin curling her rosy lips.

"I've always wanted a knight in shining armor to come to my rescue," Agatha said huskily, then started as if poked with a pin. "Oh, my God!" she blurted, pressing a hand to her mouth. Suddenly she started off through the pines, pulling him along with her. "What am I thinking of! Pa and my sisters are in big trouble. You've got to help them, too."

"Whoa, there," Fargo said, trying to tug his arm from her clinging grasp. "What is this all about? I don't like to go into a bear's den unless I know what's in there."

"Four of Haddock's men jumped us," Agatha said. She jerked a thumb over her shoulder. "Those two will be out for hours, but the other two might have their grimy hands on the rest of my family by now. You have to help them."

"I have to do no such thing," Fargo countered. He dug in his heels, bringing himself and Agatha to a halt. "Not unless you tell me what's going on. Why are these men after you?"

"They're not after me, dunderhead," Agatha said impatiently. "They're after my pa."

"Why?"

"There's no time to explain, damn it!" Agatha said, hauling on his arm again. "If we don't hurry it will be too late. My pa and my sisters will be killed and their blood will be on your hands!"

As if to prove her right, from several hundred yards to the north came the crack of a revolver, three times in swift succession.

"Please!" Agatha pleaded, tears forming as she franti-

cally tried to get him to move. "Please don't let them die!"

"Oh, hell," Fargo muttered, and against his better judgment he let her lead him toward the shooting. He remembered the Sharps and almost stopped, but a strident scream from up ahead made him realize he might be too late if he went back for the rifle. So he raced alongside Agatha Jennings until he glimpsed figures moving in a clearing. Grabbing her wrist, he darted to the right behind a pine tree.

"What are you doing?" she objected. "We're not there yet."

"We're close enough," Fargo whispered. "And keep your voice down unless you want Haddock's men to hear you." He leaned out and scanned the clearing, which was situated at the base of a cliff flanking a high hill. Haddock's men were easy to spot; they were holding revolvers on a grizzled man in dirty long underwear who was kneeling between them. Nearby stood two young women, a very attractive pair in their early twenties or thereabouts, both brunettes, one thin with hair to her shoulders and the other sporting thick hair down to her thighs. They appeared terrified. The man in the long underwear was wringing his hands and glancing from one gunman to the other. He was saying something, but Skye couldn't make out the words.

"Do something!" Agatha goaded. "They'll kill him at any moment!"

"Hold your horses," Fargo muttered, trying to come up with a plan, a way to distract Haddock's men so he could get the drop on them. It would be less of a headache to simply shoot them, but he wanted to learn what Snake Haddock was after, and they might be persuaded to tell him. The name Haddock had come up a few times in his travels, always in connection with one grisly crime or another. If Agatha's pa had been a member of the outlaw gang that rode with Haddock, then old man Jennings had to have a heart as black as the ace of spades. And what did that say about his daughters? "I want you to run around to the east side of the clearing. Stay hidden until you see me wave, then step into the open."

"And do what?"

"Nothing. Just stand there."

Agatha looked at him as if he was out of his mind. "Are you sure you know what you're doing? I don't want to get myself killed."

"I need an edge," Fargo informed her. "If I pop out of nowhere, they might start shooting and your family could get caught in the cross fire. Do you want that to happen?"

"No. Of course not. But what good will showing myself to them do?"

"It will buy me a second or two," Fargo said testily, annoyed at having his judgment questioned. "Don't worry about your hide. They want you alive, or Murdock and Wolney would have shot you."

She gazed toward the clearing and nodded. "Oh. Now I understand."

"And remember to keep your eyes on me until you're in position. I'll be making my way closer."

"You do know what you're doing," Agatha said and smirked. Impulsively, she pressed her body to his and gave him a kiss on the cheek, her soft, moist lips clinging to his skin for an instant before she dashed off to do his bidding.

Fargo watched her, admiring the lush curves that hinted at delights beyond measure. If he was any judge of women, Agatha Jennings would be a wildcat in bed. He put such thoughts aside at a sharp cry from the clearing.

One of Haddock's men had slugged Jennings, and the old man was now lying on his side, rubbing his jaw. The daughter with the long hair, her fists clenched, wanted to tear into the culprit but was being held back by her sister.

Fargo padded nearer, exercising all his wilderness savvy, moving as stealthily as an Indian, pausing once to stick the throwing knife into its sheath inside his boot. He kept close track of Agatha, worried the two outlaws would spot her yellow dress. But they never so much as glanced at the forest. All they were concerned about was her father.

Why had Snake Haddock sent them? What did Haddock care if a gang member decided to call it quits? The outlaw trail was brutally hard, what with the outlaws always being on the run, always having to look over their shoulders, never having a safe place to call home. Once their identities became known to the law, their days were numbered. The smart ones realized their mistake early and got out while they could. Most wound up with a fatal case of lead poisoning. A few, a very few, made a career of it and lived to old age. Jennings must be in his fifties, an old-timer by frontier standards, well past his prime. If he wanted to hang up his guns, why should Haddock mind?

Soon he could hear the conversation between Jennings and the hard cases.

"—what we came for, Hugh. Snake told us he wanted you alive, but he didn't say we couldn't break a few bones if we were of a mind," a beefy man in a black hat said.

"I don't know what you're talkin' about," Jennings responded. "Snake is loco if he thinks I did."

"The boss is a lot of things but loco isn't one of them. If he says you did, you did."

Fargo reached a tree near the clearing and stopped. Agatha was to the east, expectantly staring at him. A flick of a hand was his signal, and she quickly edged closer to the open space. Neither of the outlaws noticed her until she walked a half-dozen feet from the trees. Then they both did and whirled, their revolvers leveled.

"Agatha!" the man in the black hat declared. "What are you doing back? I thought you were heading for the hills."

"I came to my senses, Dorn, and came back to be with my family," she answered, giving her father and sisters a reassuring smile.

"Where's Murdock and Wolney?" Dorn asked suspiciously.

"I gave those yacks the slip. Between the two of them they don't have the brains God gave a turnip."

The gunmen laughed.

"Ain't that the truth!" Dorn said good-naturedly. "Why, Wolney is the dumbest critter this side of the Divide. Once we held up some miners and they showed their grit by fighting back. That fool Wolney drew his six-shooter and took to firing, but all the chambers were empty. He'd forgotten to reload his gun the night before when he was cleaning it. About got himself killed."

By then Fargo had taken three long strides, his soles making no noise on the soft grass. He was a couple of yards from them when he halted and announced, "Howdy, gents. Don't make any sudden moves. I never forget to reload my gun." He saw them go rigid. Their backs were to him so he couldn't see their faces, but he could tell by the tone of Dorn's reply that there would be gunplay.

"Who are you, mister? Why are you throwing a hand in this?"

"I'm the one who taught Murdock and Wolney some manners," Skye said in the hope these two wouldn't try anything if they knew their companions were out of commission. "And I'll do the same to you if you don't throw your hog-legs down right this minute."

Dorn snorted. "We're from Missouri, stranger."

With that, both gunmen whirled.

2

So much for prying answers out of them. The Trailsman fired at Dorn first, squeezing the trigger just as the beefy outlaw completed his turn, the slug catching Dorn in the temple and causing him to stagger backward. In the blink of an eye Fargo squeezed off another shot, striking the other man in the chest over the heart. Haddock's men both hit the ground at the same time, Dorn's mouth working convulsively, the second man twitching a few times. Then both lay still.

The Jennings clan gawked.

Fargo stepped over to the bodies, making certain. He collected their guns and slid his own into its holster.

"Much obliged, mister," Hugh Jennings said, pushing upright. "I thought I was goner. Those two were as mean as rattlers."

"I heard Dorn say they weren't going to kill you," Fargo reminded him, and added to get a reaction, "in fact, he was downright friendly to Agatha. I got the idea you were all well acquainted."

Hugh cleared his throat and cast a nervous look at his eldest. "We rode together a while back, but all that changed."

"You mean when you were riding with Snake Haddock?" Fargo innocently inquired.

Jennings puffed up his cheeks and huffed like a fish out of water, then turned on Agatha. "What did you do, gal? Tell this jasper my life's story? Don't you have sense enough not to blab everything you know to total strangers?"

"There's no call for you to get all hot under the collar, Pa. He overheard Murdock and me talking," she replied, advancing to her sisters. "Are you two all right?"

18

Both women nodded. "They hardly paid attention to us," said the thin one.

"Except to tell us to butt out or have our heads busted," chimed in the lovely girl with the long hair.

Agatha walked up to Dorn. One second she was standing over him, calm and collected. The next she underwent a startling transformation, her features contorting in feral anger as she gave the dead man a savage kick. "Serves you right for not leaving well enough alone!" she snapped, then instantly composed herself and smoothed her dress. "Now then," she said, facing Fargo. "In all the excitement I don't believe you gave me your name."

"Skye Fargo, at your service, ma'am," he said, slightly disturbed at the way she had changed so drastically from one moment to the next.

"Fargo, you say?" Hugh Jennings said, blinking in surprise. "Not the one they call the Trailsman?"

"That's me," Fargo admitted, seeing no reason to hide the fact. For better or worse, he was one of the best-known frontiersmen in the entire West.

Not that he went out of his way to add to the tales being told. But deep within him burned an unquenchable wanderlust, a powerful hankering to see all that he could see and experience whatever came along. It was why he constantly crisscrossed the country, always seeking what lay over the next horizon. And America being what it was, a young nation containing millions of square miles of uncharted land teeming with untold dangers, he constantly ran into trouble.

Somewhere along the line talk had started, and now he was a frequent topic of conversation in many a saloon and tavern. It was why so many folks knew about his exploits and why hard cases gave him a wide berth when he came down a street. "Don't tangle with the Trailsman," the saying went, "unless you're looking to be planted six feet under."

"Jesus," Hugh said softly. "Of all the luck." He mustered a smile and came forward, his gnarled right hand extended. "It's a good thing you came along when you did, Mr. Fargo. Yes, sir. The good Lord was watchin' out for my girls and me."

Fargo shook, noting the exceptional strength the old-timer possessed. Looks could be deceiving, he noted.

Hugh Jennings might be pushing sixty, but he was as spry and wiry as a twenty-year-old. "Glad I could be of help," he said.

The daughters joined them, and Agatha made the introductions. Constance was the name of the skinny one, Sophia the sister with the long tresses. Neither was particularly shy about taking his hand. Sophia, especially, made a point of roving her sparkling brown eyes from the crown of his hat to the scuffed tips of his boots and then licking her lips as if she was about to indulge in a sumptuous feast.

"I'm right glad to make your acquaintance, big man," she said huskily, fastening her gaze on a prominent point below his belt buckle. "You have no idea how starved we are for company out here in these godforsaken mountains. I'm so bored I could cry."

"We wouldn't want that," Fargo said, aware their father was scrutinizing him intently. He gave a nod and started to turn. "Now if you'll excuse me, ladies."

"Whoa, there!" Sophia exclaimed, grabbing his wrist. "You're not running off on us, are you?"

Hugh Jennings took a step closer. "I should hope he isn't, girl. I'm lookin' forward to havin' him join us for supper. It's the least we can do to repay his kindness." He nodded toward the cliff. "What do you say, Mr. Fargo? Will you join us? We're having venison stew and you'll kick yourself if you pass it up. My Connie is a wizard at fixin' victuals."

Skye suddenly realized there was a shallow grotto at the base of the sheer rocky height. A number of saddles, bags, and packs were piled along the rear wall. To the left of the opening were six horses tethered to bushes.

"Please come!" Sophia requested eagerly, rubbing up against him. "We promise to show you a good time."

"I reckon I can," Fargo said. Truth to tell, he *was* starved. And since he had missed bagging an elk to lend them a hand, it was fitting they treat him to a meal. He smiled down at Sophia, then saw Agatha glaring at the two of them. "I'll be back after I fetch my gear and check on Murdock and Wolney."

"They're still alive?" Hugh asked in alarm and glanced at Agatha. "Why didn't you tell me, girl?"

"They're out to the world, Pa. Fargo about broke their skulls wide open."

"I don't care. You should have said something," Hugh said irritably, gazing fearfully into the forest.

"What does it matter?" Fargo said. "In a few minutes I'll have them trussed up so tight they won't be able to scratch themselves, let alone hurt your family."

"That's a good idea," Hugh said. He motioned for Fargo to be on his way. "You'd better get goin'. If they come around before you get there, there will be hell to pay. The sooner you have those murderers tied up good and proper, the safer I'll feel for my daughters."

Fargo nodded at the three lovelies and began to retrace his steps. He hadn't gone five feet when Agatha materialized on his right side and hooked her arm around his. "What do you think you're doing?" he demanded.

"I'm tagging along in case you need help."

"You stay put. If they have come around, they'll be out for blood. It's too dangerous for you to go with me."

"I can take care of myself."

Stopping, Fargo glanced at Hugh, counting on her father to back him up. No caring parent would ever let a cherished son or daughter foolishly risk their life. "Tell her," he said.

Hugh gave the impression of being genuinely puzzled. "Tell her what?" he responded.

"That she can't go."

"Shucks, mister. I ain't been able to tell that girl what to do since she was knee high to a colt. Aggie has always done as she pleases without so much as a by-your-leave. If she wants to tag along with you, I'm afraid you're stuck with her. And I wouldn't fret myself, if I were you. She's a regular tomcat."

As much as Fargo would have liked to argue the point, he didn't want to delay any longer. He kept thinking about the Sharps and chided himself for leaving it behind. If, by some miracle, the two hard cases were back on their feet, they might spot it. And he didn't want to lose that gun. While a pistol was fine for close-in fighting and slaying small game, keeping hostiles at bay or downing deer or elk or buffalo required a gun with more stopping power. In that respect a Sharps was ideal for dropping man or beast. The powerful wallop from a .52

caliber Sharps could lift a grown man from his feet and kill a bull buffalo at a distance of eight hundred yards or better. Some said it was the best gun ever made. He felt undressed without his, like a man going to a fancy ball wearing just his pants.

"Don't bother yourself about these bodies, neither," Hugh went on, jabbing a finger at the dead men. "My girls and me will take care of planting them." He nodded at the two revolvers held in Fargo's left hand. "And you can leave those here if you want. We might need them if there are more of Haddock's men about."

Unwilling to waste another moment, Skye gave the revolvers to Hugh without comment, then wheeled and hastened toward the tree where he had left the Sharps. Agatha stayed by his side the whole time, keeping her mouth shut and her eyes alert for trouble. His unerring sense of direction, honed by years of finding his way across territory no other white men had ever visited, enabled him to make a beeline to the exact pine where he had propped the rifle. There he found his worst fear realized.

The Sharps was gone.

He had approached silently and seen no sign of either Murdock or Wolney anywhere along the way. Now, his Colt in hand, he walked past the tree to where the two men had been lying. They were gone, too. A small puddle of blood marked the spot where Wolney had lain.

Scouring the ground, The Trailsman found their tracks. The footprints told the whole story. Murdock had revived first and brought Wolney around. Probably looking for Fargo and Agatha, Murdock had walked in a small circle. It was then the outlaw spied the rifle; his boot prints were as plain as day at the base of the pine.

"What's the matter?" Agatha whispered. "You look like you just lost your best friend."

Fargo told her about the rifle while examining the sign. He found where Murdock and Wolney had left. Oddly, instead of making for the cliff they had headed to the east. Where were they going? "Let's go," he said and hurried in pursuit. He didn't dare go as fast as he would have liked. For one thing, he didn't want to leave Agatha behind. For another, Murdock might be lying in wait with the Sharps, and he didn't want to blunder into an ambush.

The trail led along the base of the mountain Fargo had been on earlier when he was hunting the elk, and into a ravine. Hoof prints showed where four horses had been ground-hitched. All four were now gone, two being led by Murdock. "Damn," Skye said, sliding his Colt into his holster.

"They'll go fetch Snake and the rest of Haddock's wild bunch," Agatha predicted. "Murdock said they were going to send someone after that bastard as soon as he got me back to the grotto."

"How many men ride with Haddock?"

"I don't rightly know. There used to be eleven back when Pa was part of the band. That was three months ago, though. We heard he added a few since then."

Fargo didn't like the odds. He debated whether to try and overtake Murdock and Wolney before they rejoined the gang or whether to stick with the Jennings clan. As if she were a mind reader, Agatha made a request that decided the matter for him.

"With Snake on the way, we'll have to high-tail it out of here. Pa doesn't know these mountains very well. We could sure use your help. How about being our guide?"

He looked at her. "Do you have any idea how far off Haddock and his men are?"

"Murdock said it would take Snake two days to get here."

"Good," Fargo said, pleased. In two days he'd have the family well on its way eastward to Fort Benton. Even if the outlaws were coming from that direction, he should be able to avoid them by swinging a bit to the south. He started for the mouth of the ravine when suddenly Agatha darted in front of him, blocking his path.

"What's your rush, big man?" she asked, her hands clasped behind her back, her body swaying suggestively.

"I have to get my horse."

Agatha grinned impishly. "It can wait awhile, can't it?" She brazenly reached out and rested her fingertips on his belt buckle. "My pa won't be expecting us back for a spell. Why not take advantage of the situation?"

"You don't believe in beating around the bush, do you?"

23

"Nope," Agatha said, inching nearer, her gaze lingering on his broad shoulders. "And in case you're wondering, it doesn't matter that we hardly know one another. When I see something I like, I go after it." She paused, chuckling. "And I like you, Trailsman. I truly do. You're about as handsome a man as I've ever laid eyes on."

Skye felt her press against him, felt her breasts mash into his chest and her hand drift lower to lightly stroke his stirring manhood. A lump formed in his throat. She was artfully fueling the flames of his lust, and he had never been one to say no to a lady who delighted in sensual pleasure. His hands came up and cupped her buttocks. What did he have to lose? For the time being the outlaws weren't a threat, and the Ovaro would be safe.

Agatha tilted her head up and licked her delectable lips. "I see you're warming up to my notion," she said, grinning wickedly.

Fargo kissed her. Her mouth was as soft as a down-filled pillow, her tongue as smooth as silk. He brought a hand around to her breasts and massaged them through the yellow dress, enjoying the way they swelled and the nipples hardened.

"Mmmmmmm," Aggie moaned. "Nice."

His other hand slid between their bodies to touch the mound at the junction of her thighs. She willingly parted her legs, allowing him access to her innermost core. Slowly, tantalizing her, he eased his hand between her legs. The heat from her slit warmed his fingers, and he eagerly hiked her dress high enough to reach underneath. Her underthings posed no obstacle. In seconds his fingers were caressing her nether lips.

"I knew you'd be good!" she cooed, arching her spine when he inserted a forefinger into her slick tunnel. "Oh, yes! Do more, lover!"

His tongue licked a path from her mouth to the bottom of her neck. Working swiftly, he unbuttoned the top of her dress and soon had her breasts exposed to his admiring gaze. Her nipples thrust outward, inviting attention, so he placed his lips on one and flicked with his tongue. Agatha arched her spine again, her hips grinding into him, her warm breath fanning his ear.

"Like that! Just like that!"

Fargo went from breast to breast, giving each a thorough treatment. All the while his finger was busy, sliding in and out of her furnace. Her moist walls constricted with each stroke, hinting at the ecstasy in store for him once he replaced his finger with his organ. For minutes he went on in the same fashion, until she was groaning and pumping herself up and down in rhythm to his strokes. Then he scooped her into his arms, stepped behind a boulder near the ravine wall, and gently deposited her on the bare earth.

The dress swirled around her hips, revealing her glorious legs and thighs. She smiled and curled a finger to beckon him down by her side.

Fargo removed his gun belt, placed it within easy reach, and knelt. It took a minute to take off her underclothes, and then he descended onto her twin peaks again, letting his mouth relish the taste of her velvety globes. Some women, he had learned, were more aroused by having their breasts massaged than others. Agatha enjoyed it immensely, her skin becoming hot to the touch, her body twisting and squirming in passionate abandon.

"Put it in me," she said breathlessly.

Not yet, Fargo thought. He wanted to draw out her delight until she was delirious with desire. Only then would he satisfy her fully. His mouth and fingers plied her yielding flesh, causing her thighs to quiver and her hands to grip his hair so hard it hurt. His hat hit the ground to one side.

"Come on, big man," Agatha pleaded. "What are you waiting for?"

The urgency in her tone pleased him. She was almost ready. He began poking her hole with two fingers rather than one, increasing her sensations. Her teeth bit into his right shoulder and her nails dug into his back.

A minute went by. Aggie was puffing like a steam engine when at last he lowered his pants and entered her. She gasped, her red lips parted seductively, her legs clamping around him to hold him fast. "You wanted it," he said. "Here it is."

At his first stroke she bucked into the air and gripped his shoulders. "Aaahhhhhh! Pound me, Fargo! Pound me good!"

Fargo put his palms on her shoulders to hold her down, then rammed into her again and again and again, his manhood throbbing, his temples drumming to the beat of his racing pulse. His skin was on fire, his body tingling with vibrant expectancy.

Agatha held onto his elbows, her hips rising to meet his own, her eyelids fluttering as her enjoyment mounted. "Ohhh! Ohhh!" she panted, then tossed her head from side to side, the tip of her tongue jutting between her lips.

He gave it all he had, driving into her to the hilt, filling her womanhood completely. On and on he went until she suddenly went berserk, flailing and kicking as her buttocks bumped up and down and her inner juices spurted all over his rigid pole. She came and came. Then, at the moment she started to coast down from the sexual heights of pure rapture, he let himself go, exploding with the force of a stick of dynamite.

"Aaaiieeee!" Agatha screeched. "Skye! Skye!"

The ravine walls echoed her cries.

It was half an hour later that Fargo sat up and gave her a friendly swat on the fanny. "Time to be going," he announced, standing.

Agatha stretched languidly, then pouted. "What's your hurry, big man? There's more where that came from. I'm ready for a second ride if you are."

"I have to get my horse," he reminded her.

"Oh, pooh! Your dumb old animal can wait," Agatha said. She playfully rubbed her hand up and down his leg. "Lay back down here. I'll have you raring to go in no time."

"Maybe later," Fargo replied, picking up his gun belt. He indicated the sun, which was hovering above the western horizon. "I want to be back with your family by dark. We'll rest tonight and head out at first light."

"Head where?"

"To the closest military post, Fort Benton. The army will protect you from Haddock and his men."

"Going to Fort Benton isn't such a great idea. Pa has a price on his head. A small price, mind you, but he's a wanted man in some parts, and he won't risk being taken into custody."

"I'll talk to him about it," Fargo said as he secured his belt. "Now make yourself presentable." He adjusted the holster on his hip to allow for a smooth draw, then reclaimed his hat.

Agatha took her sweet time rearranging her clothes. She dallied, covering her breasts, cupping first one and then the other, casting sly looks at him in the obvious hope he would change his mind. When he showed no interest, she frowned and quickly finished dressing. "You have more self-control than most ten men I know," she commented sourly.

"There's a time for everything," Fargo said, and led her into the woodland beyond the ravine. The woods were alive with wildlife—squirrels scampering high in the trees, birds chirping in the branches, chipmunks racing from cover to cover in search of food and occasional rabbits spooked from their hiding places. He saw deer tracks and once, near his camp site, the prints of a grizzly. The latter bothered him. A hungry grizzly would go after anything, and he had left the Ovaro tied to a tree.

He picked up the pace and within minutes was standing in the small clearing he had chosen for his camp site. To his right flowed a gently gurgling stream, and beside it waited his dependable pinto stallion, its ears pricked, its nostrils flaring to catch Agatha's scent.

"My, what a pretty critter," she said. "I don't believe I've ever seen another horse with those type of markings. What kind is it?"

"An Ovaro," Fargo said, walking over and giving the stallion a pat on the neck. It bobbed its great head and nuzzled against him until he untied the rope and took it over to where his saddle, saddle blanket, saddlebags, and bedroll lay.

"That horse is quite attached to you," Agatha noted.

"You might say we're family."

"You're joshing me. This stallion is the only family you've got?"

"The only one that counts," Fargo said. He saddled up, fastened the bedroll in place, and coldly regarded the empty rifle scabbard. No matter what it took, he was going to get his Sharps back. The next time he ran into Murdock and Wolney he would let his Colt do his talking.

Swinging up, he gripped the reins and offered a hand to Agatha. She tittered devilishly as she settled in behind him. He found out why once they were under way and her hands strayed to his groin. "Behave yourself, woman," he growled.

"You don't fool me none. You want it again as much as I do."

Disputing the point was useless. "There will be other times." he promised.

"There had better be," Agatha said. She let go of his organ to jab him in the ribs. "And keep this in mind, big man. You're mine. Sophia and Constance aren't to touch you. If I catch you messing around with them, I'll make sure you never bed another woman as long as you live."

Fargo didn't bother to respond, but deep down he was wondering if he had made a mistake in making love to her. He had the eerie feeling she meant every word.

3

"Damn, this is tasty!" Hugh Jennings declared with his mouth crammed full of deer meat and some of the brown broth dribbling down over his grizzled chin. He smacked his lips, then wiped them with the back of his shirt sleeve. "Was I right, Fargo? Doesn't my Connie make the best dang stew this side of the Mississippi?"

"She's a fine cook," Fargo allowed, dipping a spoon into his large bowl. He was on his third helping of the savory dish and planned to have one more. Before him, suspended over the crackling fire on a metal tripod, was the huge pot in which the stew simmered.

"Thank you, sir," Constance said from her seat across the fire. Her white teeth reflected the flickering light.

Agatha, who was sitting on Fargo's left, squirmed and lowered her spoon. "I'll cook supper tomorrow night. If Skye thinks you're good, wait until he eats what I fix."

"Just don't accidentally poison the man," Sophia said and broke into laughter. Both Hugh and Connie joined in.

"I never poison anyone by accident," Agatha snapped, glaring at her buxom sibling. "And if you don't watch yourself, little sister, I'll tear your hair out by the roots."

Hugh abruptly stopped laughing. "Now don't go gettin' riled, Aggie. Sophia didn't mean nothing by what she said." He glanced at Fargo. "Think of our guest. I want all of you on your best behavior while he's with us. Savvy?"

None of the girls spoke.

"Do you understand?" Hugh bellowed, prompting all three to nod. "Good! Then I don't expect to have to bring this up again. And Aggie?"

"Yes?"

"I don't want you tryin' to go whole hog again. Your sisters have as much right as you do. We're a family, remember? We share everything." Hugh grinned. "So tomorrow night you can cook and show off for Mr. Fargo."

Fargo paused in the act of chewing. Sophia and Constance were sharing sly looks while Agatha simply sat and sulked. What was this all about? He suspected there was an underlying meaning to Hugh's words, but it couldn't be what he thought it might be. And what was this business about poisoning him? The more he got to know these people, the stranger they appeared. What the hell had he gotten himself into, anyway?

Hugh turned toward him. "Don't pay us no mind. Like any family we have our squabbles from time to time." He gestured at his daughters. "You might think raisin' girls would be easy, but I can tell you different. Girls can be just as ornery and hardheaded as boys. Sometimes they can be downright nasty."

"You seem to have done a good job," Skye said for lack of anything else to say.

"I can't take all the credit. Their ma, bless her soul, did most of the rearin' when they were small," Hugh said, leaning on an elbow. "I married late, Mr. Fargo. I was pushing thirty when I met their ma and fell head over heels in love. And Lord, was she a woman! No man ever was more proud of his wife than I was." A shadow clouded his features. "I miss her something terrible. She took a fever and passed on to her reward five years ago. . . ."

"Seven," Sophia corrected him.

"Has it really been that long? Damn. Time flies when you're in misery." Hugh toyed with his stew for a moment. "I didn't have much to do with them when they were young 'cause I was gallivanting all over the country. But when I heard tell their ma had died, I figured I should do the fatherly thing and take care of them until they get themselves hitched." He looked up. "Are you married, Fargo?"

"No."

Sophia and Constance smiled.

"Do tell," Hugh went on. "Well, don't wait too long, like I did. There's a lot to be said for married life. You get three squares a day and a warm bed to sleep in at night. It sure beats the outlaw life all hollow."

"I heard you quit Snake Haddock," Fargo said in the hope Jennings would reveal why Haddock was after him.

Hugh nodded. "I'm tryin', but the man just don't like to let any of his own go. He must figure I'll run to the law or something, which is pure crazy 'cause I'm a wanted man myself."

Fargo put more stew into his mouth and pondered. The idea that Haddock was afraid Hugh might turn him in was indeed preposterous. There was nothing Hugh could possibly tell the law that would put Snake in jeopardy. Haddock was notorious for never staying in the same place for long and never relying on the same hideout more than a few times, which was why no marshal or sheriff had yet been able to put an end to his bloody career. There was no pattern to Haddock's activities, and without a pattern the lawmen had little hope of taking him into custody or setting up an ambush to put an end to him once and for all.

"Aggie tells me you're willin' to guide us to safety," Hugh remarked. "I don't know these mountains well myself, so I'm glad for the help."

"What brought you out here in the first place?" Skye asked.

"I just wanted to spend some time alone with my gals."

Fargo didn't believe it for a minute, not with so many hostile Indians living in the region. Hugh had to know the Blackfeet and Bloods killed whites on sight. There had to be another reason, a reason that justified exposing the three women to such great danger.

"There's just one thing," Hugh said.

"What?"

"Aggie says you want to take us to Fort Benton. I'm afraid that's out of the question. I can't take the chance of havin' some busybody recognize me and the law slappin' leg irons on me." Hugh leaned forward. "You can see my point, can't you?"

"Do you have a better idea?"

"As a matter of fact, I do," Hugh said. "How about if you take us southeast until we hit the plains. From there we can go any direction we like."

"I can do that if you want," Fargo said.

"We'll be obliged," Hugh stated, and gazed at each of his daughters. "How does St. Louis strike you three? I know you're sick and tired of livin' in the wild."

"St. Louis!" Sophia practically shouted, sitting upright so quickly she spilled some of her stew on her lap.

"Do you mean it, Pa?" Connie asked.

Agatha was also excited. She threw down her empty bowl and ran over to her father to give him a hug and kiss him on the cheek. "At last you're coming to your senses! Don't you see I was right all the time? We'll fare better in a big city where we can blend in with all the other folks."

"I admit it. I should have listened to you sooner," Hugh said, giving her a peck on the chin. "You always have been clever like a fox. Ma liked to say you could trick a starving man out of his last bit of bread."

Her own mother said that? Fargo reflected, leaning on a knee so he could ladle more stew into his bowl. And it was supposed to be a compliment! He saw Constance staring at him. When he returned her gaze, she winked and casually hiked the hem of her dress a few inches to display her dainty ankle.

"I can't wait to get to St. Louis," Sophia said. "To be able to take long, hot baths again, to wear new, pretty dresses all the time and to have a different beau every night! That's the kind of life for me."

"Me, too," Connie said.

"Have you ever been there, Skye?" Sophia asked.

"A few times."

"Is it everything they say it is? As grand as New York City, as glorious as Paris? Do rich folks really ride around in fine carriages pulled by white horses? Are there lots of dress shops and fancy hotels and restaurants?"

"I seem to recollect there are," Fargo answered, sitting down again.

"Are there opera houses and theaters?" Constance inquired.

"Yes," Fargo confirmed.

"And lots and lots of eligible men?" Sophia added.

Hugh cackled and slapped his thigh. "You have to forgive my brood, Mr. Fargo. They ain't seen much of big city life, but they've heard a passel of stories from those who have. Why, they'll wear your ears out askin' about life there if you let them."

From outside the grotto came a loud whinny.

Fargo was on his feet in an instant, listening for any sounds that might be carried on the light breeze. That had been the Ovaro. His hand fell to his Colt and he moved toward the entrance.

"Trouble, you figure?" Hugh asked apprehensively.

"Could be nothing," Fargo said. "I'll check." He stepped into the night and moved to the right so his body wouldn't be silhouetted by the firelight within. The horses all had their heads up and were peering into the murky forest to the west. Something was out there, a cougar or that grizzly perhaps. He walked to the pinto and draped his arm over its neck.

Deep in the woods an owl hooted. In the distance a wolf howled and was answered by another.

Fargo walked a few feet into the darkness, straining his senses to catch the faintest noise or the slightest hint of movement. So it was he heard the soft footfalls behind him well before he scented sweet perfume and turned to find Sophia sashaying toward him. "You should stay inside," he advised.

"Whatever for? Everyone knows Injuns don't prowl around at night, and Snake won't be able to get here for a couple of days. I'm safe," she said, halting so close to him that the tips of her breasts brushed his buckskins. Her mouth curved upward. "Or am I?"

"Does Agatha know you're out here?"

"Who cares if she does or she doesn't? I'm not scared of her," Sophia said, putting a hand on his chest. "And don't tell me a big, strong man like you is afraid of getting her mad?"

"I just don't want to cause trouble. We'll have a hard enough time as it is without fighting among ourselves."

Sophia chuckled. "You don't know us very well. We've been at each other's throats since we were born." She leaned into him, her lips inches from his own, her warm breath tingling his nostrils. "It seems like ages since I last had a man. Why don't you remind me what it's like?"

Before Fargo could do a thing she flattened her lips against his and lifted his left hand to her breast. Her tongue probed his mouth. He felt his organ rise to attention. The hot meal had done wonders for his tired body, and he would have hitched her dress then and there if not for an unexpected interruption.

"Fargo?" Hugh Jennings called from the grotto.

In a flash Sophia stepped back and brushed at her long hair with her hand. "We're over here, Pa," she replied.

Fargo scanned the trees and turned to gaze up at the top of the cliff, which was a stark, jagged black line against the backdrop of stars. Was it his imagination or had something moved up there? His eyes narrowed but he saw nothing to verify his fleeting impression.

"Is anything wrong?" Hugh asked as he came toward them, a rifle in his left hand.

"I guess not," Skye said. The horses were no longer staring at the woods so whatever had been out there must have moved on.

"Good," Hugh said, and hefted his rifle. "I got to thinkin'. Maybe it would be smart for us to stand guard. I know Haddock isn't anywhere close to us, but it would make the girls sleep easier if they knew we were keepin' watch over them. How about it? We'll split the night in half and I'll go first if you want."

Although Fargo would rather have slept the whole night through, his gut instincts told him to go along with the plan. There was a possibility a mountain lion or grizzly just might go after the horses. And, too, there was something about the Jennings clan that wasn't quite right. He couldn't put his finger on why, but he felt vaguely uneasy about letting down his guard for any length of time. Perhaps the less he slept, the better. "All right," he said.

"Let me get a cup of coffee and I'll be right back out," Hugh said. He hastened off.

"Now where were we?" Sophia asked the instant they were alone. She glued her warm form to his and clasped his hands. "He'll take five minutes if I know him. How about if we fool around some more?"

In all his travels Fargo had rarely met women as bold and shameless as the Jennings girls. All they had on their minds was sex. Under different circumstances he would have enjoyed their refreshing attitude, but now he was a bit irritated. If things kept going the way they were, the sisters wouldn't give him a moment's peace. And what with Agatha's threat, the talk about poison, and his suspicion that Hugh was hiding something, he needed to keep his wits about him at all times.

"Well?" Sophia urged.

"You want to fool around? Fine," Fargo said gruffly, and abruptly shoved his right hand between her legs and clamped a hand on her innermost recesses. She stiffened, gasped, and clutched his shoulders.

"Oh, God! You don't believe in wasting any time, do you?"

"No," Fargo growled, rubbing his fingers back and forth, feeling the heat of the friction added to the heat from her core. Sophia closed her eyes and licked her lips.

"UUuuuummmm. You're making me wet."

Despite himself, Fargo was fully aroused. He felt the familiar tightening in his loins and glanced at the mouth of the grotto. No one was there. What were the other women doing? Like Sophia had said, who the hell cared? He suddenly gripped her by the front of her dress and hauled her toward the base of the cliff, working his way to the left until they were halfway between the horses and the pines. She made no attempt to resist, and when he stopped she threw her arms around him and molded her mouth to his.

He had his back to the cliff face so he could keep an eye on the grotto, the clearing, and the trees. With a jerk he raised her dress to her hips and plunged both hands into her underclothes. His fingers found her slit. Without preliminaries, he rammed his middle finger into her hole. His thumb found her passion knob.

"Sweet Jesus!" Sophia husked, leaning her forehead on his chest. "Take it slow. I don't want to rush this."

"Too bad." Fargo grinned, adding two more fingers, his hand becoming drenched in her warm juices. He slid his other hand out and reached for his pants, when he heard a light patter on his hat that resembled the sound of falling raindrops. Only there wasn't a cloud in the moonlit sky. The next second a small stone or pebble struck his left shoulder and he realized what was happening. Yanking his fingers out, he gripped Sophia about the waist and took several swift strides, then spun and scoured the cliff rim.

"What the hell?" Sophia complained, her dress enfolding her legs again. "Don't stop now."

"Quiet," Skye commanded. "There's someone or something up there."

"There is?" she said skeptically. "How do you know?"

There was no need for Fargo to explain because at that very moment a rock hit the ground with a resounding crack. Then, from far overhead, came a faint scraping noise.

"Oh!" Sophia exclaimed.

Try as he might, Fargo couldn't pinpoint the cause. It might be an animal, in which case he was worried over nothing. But if it wasn't, then he had better have eyes in the back of his head come daylight. There was a good chance a war party had found them. Perhaps a Blackfoot or a Blood was keeping an eye on their camp. If so, the Indians would bide their time and strike when they were most vulnerable to attack.

He grabbed Sophia's wrist and made for the grotto. No further noises punctuated the night, and they reached the horses just as Hugh emerged, carrying a tin cup of steaming coffee. "We may not be alone," he declared, letting go of Sophia. She promptly hurried inside.

"What makes you think so?"

Fargo told him, surveying the cliff the whole time. "If it is hostiles, I doubt they'll try anything before daylight. But you never know."

"Maybe all they want is our horses," Hugh said. "Injuns are always on the lookout for prime horseflesh."

"Maybe," Fargo said. Deep down, he doubted such was the case. A war party wouldn't settle for just stealing their animals when scalps, guns, and women were also ripe for the taking. "You'd better be on your toes while you're keeping guard. Don't let yourself fall asleep for a second. That's all it would take for some eager brave to slit your throat from ear to ear."

Hugh nodded. "I know. I've seen Injun handiwork a few times. Once, down Tucson way, I saw a couple of prospectors after the Apaches got done with them. Their eyeballs had been ripped out, their fingers and toes chopped off, and their innards torn from their bodies." He shuddered and stared upward. "Believe you me, I'm not about to doze off."

"Wake me when it's my turn," Fargo said and went into the grotto. He looked back once to see Hugh move out of the dim glow cast by the fire. Smart man. He was convinced an old hand like Jennings wasn't likely to be caught unawares.

"Is what Sophia says true?" Agatha asked as he neared all three daughters who wore anxious expressions. "Is there someone up on the cliff?"

"Could be," Fargo said, going straight to the coffeepot. A cup or two would help him sleep lightly. Not that he was a heavy sleeper. But with the possibility of Indians lurking in the vicinity, he wanted to be able to snap awake at a moment's notice. Many a trapper and mountain man had been roused from deep sleep to find a smirking warrior standing over him and his life's blood bathing his buckskins.

Agatha stood, stepped to the rear wall, and scooped up a rifle. "I'll go first," she announced to her sisters. "Who cares to relieve me?"

"I will," Sophia said.

"That leaves me to handle the last spell," Constance added.

"Hold on," Fargo threw in. "What's this all about?" He glanced at Aggie. "Where do you think you're going?"

"To keep watch with Pa."

"He can take care of himself. You'd be safer staying in here."

"And let you and him take all the risks? Not on your life, mister. We're a family. We stick together through thick and thin. So each of us is going to help out tonight," Agatha said. "Since you're in this as much as we are, we're going to lend you a hand, too. Sophia and Connie will take turns on your watch."

Fargo's first thought was that the moment Sophia was alone with him she would try to get into his britches. And as much as he would like the opportunity to finish what she had started earlier, there was a time and a place for everything. He'd hate for a band of bloodthirsty Blackfeet to catch him with his pants down. "Thanks, but I can manage by myself."

"Four eyes and ears are better than two," Agatha responded, heading out. "We're going to do it whether you like the notion or not so you might as well go along with it."

"Don't worry," Sophia said. "All of us know how to use a gun and we're fair shots. We won't be a burden."

Much to Fargo's surprise, she proved to be right. When Hugh roused him from a fitful slumber, he walked out to find her in the inky shadows near the entrance. He moved down to the other end of the string. For the next few hours all was quiet. Sophia made no attempt to seduce him. She was relieved by Constance, who stayed vigilant until the first streaks of rosy light brightened the eastern horizon. Then Connie went inside.

Fargo made a circuit of the horses, scanned the tree line, and scrutinized the cliff from bottom to top. If there was a warrior up there the man, was well hidden. He walked to the Ovaro and began patting and rubbing it, pretending to be only interested in the stallion while the whole time he surreptitiously scoured the pines for telltale movement. All he saw was a flock of chirping sparrows, several noisy squirrels, and an owl winging its way back to its roost.

"Care for some coffee and biscuits?"

He turned. Hugh had a cup in each hand. "Don't mind if I do," he said, taking one. The first sip about scalded his mouth and he scrunched up his lips.

"Sorry. Forgot to warn you. Aggie made this batch, and she likes her coffee hot enough to melt lead." Hugh nodded at the forest. "Anything?"

"No."

"Then I reckon it's safe to pack up and be on our way. We have a lot of supplies to load on our pack animals. Will you keep an eye out while we do?"

"Someone has to."

"Good," Hugh said. "I'll be right back with those biscuits."

Fargo munched on the delicious pair Jennings brought him while the family busied themselves saddling up and tying various packs and bundles onto the two packhorses. Constantly surveying the woods and the cliff as he was, he almost missed something odd. Absently, he had observed Hugh lead one of the animals close to the grotto mouth. Then, out of the corner of his eye, he glimpsed Hugh, Aggie, and Connie lugging a wooden box to the horse. How strange, he thought, that it took all three of them to carry one small box. From the way they were stooped over, he guessed the box must be extremely heavy. They swiftly strapped it on, then draped a green blanket over it and tied that down. Hugh straightened and glanced at him, but Fargo acted as if he hadn't seen a thing. Soon they were done. The women spoke little and appeared eager to get out of there.

Fargo saddled the Ovaro, climbed up, and took the lead, making for the pines to the south. He twisted so he could check the cliff one last time, and it was well he did.

High at the top a rifle boomed.

4

Fargo felt the bullet nip at his hair. Had he not turned his head at just the right instant, his brains would have been splattered all over the Ovaro. "Go back!" he bellowed to the others as he drew the Colt. "Take cover!"

To their credit, the Jennings clan was already doing just that, with Sophia and Constance tugging the pack animals toward the grotto while Hugh and Agatha trained their rifles on the lofty heights above them.

The rifle thundered again.

This time Fargo saw a glint of sunlight off the barrel. He snapped off two quick shots, doubtful he would score but hoping to keep the rifleman pinned down for the few seconds it would take everyone to reach safety. He heard a frantic whinny and a thud and faced front barely in time to swerve aside and avoid trampling on Hugh's horse, which was down with a gaping hole in its side, thrashing wildly in its death throes. Hugh had rolled clear and was angrily returning fire.

"Take cover!" Fargo repeated, slowing and squeezing off his third shot. He fired twice more before Hugh got to the base of the cliff. Reining up next to the grotto, he jumped down and began reloading.

"Damned Injuns!" Hugh fumed, gesturing at his still thrashing horse. "That there was a fine animal. And the bastard shot it on purpose! He wasn't even tryin' to plug me."

Connie and Sophia, their backs to the cliff, were holding the reins and leads to the other animals. Aggie was pacing back and forth like a caged cougar, her thumb on the hammer of her rifle as she peered eagerly upward.

"Let that rotten polecat show himself and there will be one less redskin in this world," she growled.

Fargo did some thinking. At one time or another he'd been shot at by men using every type of gun under the sun. He could easily distinguish between the report of a rifle and a revolver. He could even tell the difference between certain kinds of rifles simply by how loud they sounded. Larger caliber guns, for instance, were invariably louder than those of lesser caliber. From the sound of the rifle on the rim, he deduced the gunman was using a Sharps, and a .52 caliber at that. And while Indians often owned rifles, few owned Sharps because white men were rarely willing to part with one. All of which brought him to a startling conclusion. "It might not be an Indian," he commented, sliding the Colt into its holster.

"Huh?" Hugh said.

"What gives you that idea?" Agatha asked.

"What if Murdock and Wolney didn't both go after Snake Haddock like we figured? What if one of them circled back to keep an eye on us until Haddock gets here?" Fargo speculated.

Agatha caught his drift. "You think Murdock is sitting up there with your own rifle?"

"Could be," Fargo said. "It explains why he went for Hugh's horse instead of Hugh. They want Hugh alive for some reason. Murdock plans to keep us pinned down until the rest of the gang shows up." He turned and started eastward. "All of you stay put. Keep the horses close to the wall so Murdock can't shoot any more of them."

"I can lend a hand," Hugh proposed.

"No thanks. It's my gun. I'll get it back," Fargo replied, breaking into a run that took him past the cliff and along the base of the hill until he had gone over two hundred yards and was on the opposite side from where he had left Jennings and his daughters. He angled upward, gliding silently over the carpet of soft grass and pine needles underfoot, counting on Murdock to be concentrating on the grotto and the open space bordering it and not the back side of the hill.

In a way Fargo knew he should be thankful. It took lots of practice before a man got to the point where he could shoot a rifle accurately each and every time. Stolen guns were no exception. And Murdock hadn't had the chance to do any practicing. If the outlaw had, Fargo would now be dead.

A new thought stopped him cold. Where had Murdock acquired ammunition for the Sharps? There had only been one round in the chamber. Yet the ambusher had fired twice. So either it wasn't Murdock or the outlaw had ammo of his own, which didn't make sense unless Murdock owned a Sharps!

Palming the Colt, he crept higher through the brush, stepping over dry twigs and branches and skirting all clearings. The higher he climbed, the steeper the slope became. When he was close to the cliff, he eased onto all fours and advanced cautiously. The final ten yards was all open ground. He hesitated before leaving the shelter of the undergrowth, wary of blundering into the rifleman's sights. There were large boulders clustered at irregular intervals along the rim, any one of which could conceal a grown man.

A tense minute went by.

Fargo took the bull by the horns and suddenly rose into a crouch, then dashed for the closest cluster. He was almost there when he heard a low cough and flattened. The sound came from somewhere to the left. Snaking in the general direction, he detected a scraping noise, as if Murdock or whoever it was had bumped the Sharps against a rock.

He crawled up next to a boulder and waited. Sooner or later the ambusher would make another noise. All he had to do was be patient and he would be able to determine exactly where the man was concealed. Patience was the key to successfully stalking anything. Even animals knew this. Mountain lions often took a half hour or more to work themselves into position to pounce on an unsuspecting deer. A bobcat would wait for ages beside a rabbit run for its prey to appear.

Close to five minutes elapsed and nothing happened. Then Fargo heard another cough that came from a point five or six yards to his left and below the rim. Gingerly, he cocked the Colt, holding the revolver under his chest to muffle the click. Bringing the Colt up to his cheek, he slowly crept around the bottom of the boulder until he was at the edge. As noiseless as a ghost, he inched out until his eyes cleared the rim.

Eight feet below on a wide ledge squatted the hard case named Murdock, Fargo's rifle clutched in his brawny hands. Beside him lay another rifle, a Sharps no less, but one adorned with brass tacks in the stock, Indian style. Also lying on the ledge was a leather ammo pouch adorned with fringe and colorful beads. Murdock was leaning forward, trying to see the base of the cliff.

Fargo extended his gun arm and would have fired, but he was afraid if he did that Murdock would pitch over the side, taking his Sharps along with him. So he aimed at the center of the outlaw's back and said, "Whether you live or not depends on what you do next."

Murdock went rigid, then chuckled. "I have to hand it to you, mister. You're good. The best I've ever run into."

"Drop my rifle," Fargo directed.

"Sure thing. Whatever you say," Murdock declared, lowering the Sharps to the ledge at his feet. "Now what?"

"You can stand, but do it real slow."

Murdock bobbed his head. "Like I told you yesterday, I know when to fold my cards." He began to rise, his arms in plain sight. "Tell me. How did you get all the way up here without me hearing you?"

For a fraction of a second Fargo was thinking of the question and not the matter at hand, which was precisely what Murdock intended. The outlaw pivoted, his right hand streaking to a revolver tucked under his belt next to the buckle. Murdock threw himself to the right as he drew, his hand a blur. But he wasn't fast enough.

Fargo squeezed the trigger, the Colt cracking and kicking in his hand, the slug tearing into the center of Murdock's chest. Astonishment lined the outlaw's face as the impact hurled him from the ledge. In pure reflex he got off a shot of his own that struck the cliff and ricocheted off. Then he plummeted, his arms and legs going limp, his mouth agape as he fell and fell until he hit the hard ground far below with a resounding thud.

Fargo slowly stood. He removed the spent cartridge from the Colt, replaced it with another from his gun belt, and twirled the revolver into his holster. A short incline took him from the rim to the ledge. He carried both rifles and the ammo pouch back up. A hail from below stopped him from going farther.

"Fargo, are you all right?"

It was Agatha, standing near Murdock. Her sisters were also there but not Hugh.

"I'm fine," Fargo shouted down. "Hang on and I'll be there in a bit." Turning, he scoured the slope on both sides. Murdock's horse had to be somewhere handy, and they needed the animal for Hugh to ride. Soon he spotted it, a large dun tied to a tree on the west side of the hill.

The animal shied at his approach, but a few soothing words and several strokes on the neck calmed its fears. He jammed Murdock's Sharps into the rifle scabbard, looped the ammo pouch over the saddle horn, and swung up, his own Sharps in the crook of his right elbow. The dun gave him no problems, and in minutes he was riding up to the grotto where the Jennings family waited.

Sophia came forward to meet him. "When I heard that shot I thought it might be Murdock shooting you. I'm glad you proved the better man."

"Thanks," Fargo said, dismounting. He handed the reins to Hugh. "Brought this for you."

"Much obliged." Jennings regarded him thoughtfully. "Never figured I'd live to see the day when any man got the better of Ira Murdock. You're every bit as good as they say you are, Trailsman."

The compliments made Fargo feel uncomfortable. He wasn't one to brag about his skill, and he disliked them making such a big deal out of a simple gunfight. All four of them were smiling at him as if he was their best friend in the whole wide world, even Aggie who by all rights should be angry that he spent time alone with Sophia last night. Why were they suddenly treating him as if he was the best friend they ever had? "Let's head out. Every minute we delay brings Snake Haddock that much closer."

Hugh headed for his dead horse. "I don't need my old saddle, but I've got some personal effects in my saddlebags and my bedroll to fetch. Then we can leave."

"I can heat you up some more coffee," Constance volunteered.

"Later," Fargo said. "Right now I just want to get out

of here." He stepped to the Ovaro and slid his Sharps into the scabbard. Gripping the horn, he tensed his legs to swing up when a hand fell lightly on his shoulder.

"Listen," Agatha whispered in his ear. "I just wanted to apologize for the way I've been acting. I have no right to stop you from courting my sisters if you're of a mind to do so." She pecked him on the cheek. "Just wanted you to know there are no hard feelings." Turning, she moved to her horse.

Suspicion flared as Fargo forked leather. What had made such a big change in Aggie? He was inclined to think the entire family had done some serious talking about him while he was up on the cliff and for some reason they had decided to butter up to him. Well, no matter how friendly they became, he wasn't about to let down his guard. He still didn't trust them completely.

Hugh transferred his effects, including his own rifle, to the dun. He removed the other Sharps, grabbed the ammo bag, and brought both over to Fargo. "I've got no need for this cannon," he said. "I've fired a Sharps before, and it bruised my shoulder something awful. Do you want it?"

Fargo almost said no. But a second rifle would be useful if Haddock's bunch overtook them. "I suppose," he replied, bending down to take the gun and the pouch. He tapped the stock, then ran his fingers over the brass tacks. "Did Murdock live with Indians at one time?"

"Hell, no," Hugh said and snickered. "Murdock hated Injuns. He got that there Sharps from an army scout he killed. Only had it a short while."

Fargo stared at the rifle, trying to recall if he had ever met the owner. He knew many of the scouts quite well. They were a hardy, lusty breed, the kind a man wanted by his side in a pinch. "This army scout have a name?" he asked, glad he had killed Murdock. It was possible the son of a bitch had murdered one of his friends.

"I didn't know the man. I didn't know any of them," Hugh said and turned to go.

"Them?"

Hugh halted in midstride and glanced over his shoulder, blinking rapidly in apparent surprise. "Did I say them?" he responded, his tone oddly strained. "I meant to say him. I didn't know him." He grinned and kept going.

Fargo didn't believe Jennings for a second. But what did it mean? Had the Haddock gang raided a military post? He doubted it. Not even Snake Haddock would be that crazy. The army would hunt Haddock down and exterminate his lawless band to the last man.

As Hugh climbed on the dun, Fargo twisted and wedged the spare Sharps into his bedroll. The extra ammunition went into his saddlebags. Finally, with a wave of his hand, he led the way into the trees. Hugh, he noticed, took the lead to the horse bearing the heavy wooden box. In light of what Hugh had just told him, he was more curious than ever to learn what was in there. At the first opportunity he planned to have a look at it.

Two hours of steady travel to the southeast brought them to the north bank of a swiftly flowing stream. Fargo called a break to water the animals and to allow the women to stretch their legs. No one had spoken much since leaving the grotto, but as soon as they stopped the sisters began chatting about the wonderful things in store for them in St. Louis. Fargo walked the Ovaro to the stream and idly leaned on the saddle while the pinto drank.

"Sometimes my girls can be worse than brood hens," Hugh remarked, strolling over. "They'll talk your ears off if you let them." He stretched, then scratched his chin. "Women are like that, ain't they?"

"Sometimes," Fargo said.

"Still, they give a man reason for livin'," Hugh went on. "I know their ma sure turned my head the first time I laid eyes on her. Talk about pretty! I only wish I'd had the brains to spend more time to home instead of gallivantin' all over creation."

"Some men are made to wander."

"Yep. True. But most have the horse sense not to live outside the law like I did." Hugh frowned. "If I had it to do all over again I'd do it different. How about you?"

"I have no complaints."

"You're happy with your life?"

Fargo nodded.

"Then you're one of the few people who will own up to it. Most are downright miserable, stuck doing work they hate or married to women who nag them to death," Hugh said. He stared at his girls. "I was never very happy on the outlaw trail, but things are about to change. My daughters and me are going to have a high old time in St. Louis. We'll buy us a place that would make a king proud."

"That takes money," Fargo noted.

Hugh took to blinking again. "Not a mansion or anything like that, you understand. I meant just a real nice place my girls and me can call home."

"It seems to me that your girls are about ready to fly the coop," Fargo said. "They won't stay single long in a big city like St. Louis."

"That's what I'm countin' on," Hugh said and chuckled. "I'm hopin' all three of 'em will latch onto nice rich fellas and do their pa proud." He strolled off to join his daughters.

The stallion lifted its head, water dripping from its mouth, and Fargo squatted to dip his hand in the stream. His gaze roved over a mountain half a mile to the south, and in doing so he spied a brief flicker of bright light. Was it the sun reflected off a gun barrel? He watched for over a minute, but the flicker wasn't repeated. If there was someone on that mountain, it couldn't be Snake Haddock. The outlaws were coming from the east. Indians, perhaps? "Mount up," he commanded, rising.

"Already?" Agatha responded. "Can't we take another ten minutes to rest?"

"I want to cover a lot of miles before nightfall," Fargo said. "You can rest then."

Agatha opened her mouth to protest, but her father cut her short. "Now, now, Aggie. Mr. Fargo knows best. Do you want Snake to catch us?"

"Maybe it would be best. I could stick a knife in his ribs and end this once and for all."

"Stickin' knives in folks isn't very ladylike. You have to start actin' proper if you want to fit in with the high society types in St. Louis."

"Sorry, Pa. I'll keep trying."

Skye crossed the stream at a shallow point, waited for the others to imitate his example, then assumed the lead. He repeatedly scanned the mountain but saw no cause for alarm. The miles gradually fell behind them. Overhead the blazing sun ascended to its zenith and arced toward the western horizon. Wildlife was everywhere—deer, elk, hawks, eagles, even a few buffalo.

Hugh rode up alongside the Ovaro. "Do you figure it will be safe to do some huntin' for our supper? We have plenty of jerky, but after all this ridin' a steak or stew would really hit the spot."

"Shots can be heard for miles if the wind is right," Fargo remarked.

"I know. But Snake ain't close enough yet. I feel it in my bones."

"There are always Indians to worry about."

"I haven't seen any sign. Have you?"

Fargo looked him in the eyes. "Weren't you the one who said I know best? If I'm to get you to the plains in one piece, you'll do as I say or go your own way."

"Don't get testy on me," Hugh said. "If you'll settle for jerky, so will we. A few days of roughin' it won't hurt us none." He turned the dun to go back with his daughters, tugging on the lead to make the packhorse cooperate.

Although Fargo was tempted to glance at the blanket covering the box, he didn't. To do so might make Hugh or the women suspicious. He stared straight ahead, mentally reviewing the layout of the countryside, trying to think of a likely spot to make camp for the night. He'd been through the region they were entering once or twice before, and each landmark was branded into his memory. It was one of the things that made him as good at what he did as Joseph Walker or Jim Bridger. All the great trailblazers had an uncanny ability to remember every detail of the country through which they passed.

They would need a camp site with water and grass for the horses—somewhere sheltered from the strong winds that frequently cropped up. And somewhere an enemy couldn't get at them without being detected.

He found exactly what he was looking for as the sun touched the distant skyline. Three years ago he had bedded down overnight at the same place and recalled it well—a crystal clear creek gurgling between two jagged peaks in a narrow pass few knew about. They had to climb for forty minutes to reach the pass, but the effort was well worth it in his estimation. High grass lined both sides of the creek. And a single sentry, by moving back and forth from one end of the pass to the other, a distance of only twenty-five yards, could watch both approaches.

"Lord, it's about time," Sophia declared when he called a halt. "We haven't done much riding for a week, and my bottom is as sore as it used to be when I was a little girl and pa paddled me for misbehaving."

"Spare the rod and spoil the child," Hugh said. "That's what people say."

Fargo slid to the ground beside the creek. In the soft mud at the water's edge he saw the fresh prints of a huge mountain lion where the roaming cat had crouched to get a drink. "We'd better tie the horses tight tonight," he advised, pointing at the prints.

Each of them examined the tracks. Then Hugh put his daughters to work gathering wood in a small stand of pines at the north end of the pass. "We'll need a lot of branches for our fire if we're to keep a big blaze going all night," he concluded. "If the mountain lion is still hereabouts, it'll think twice before it attacks any of our animals."

"Keep the fire small," Fargo corrected him. "This high up a big blaze can be seen from ten miles off or better." He pulled the Sharps free. "The only way to be safe is to keep watch all night. I'll take the first shift this time."

"Damn," Hugh muttered. "I was lookin' forward to gettin' a good night's sleep."

"We'll take turns, too," Agatha said.

"Yeah. We can do our fair share to help," Connie declared.

Fargo didn't waste his breath debating the issue. He now knew the Jennings women well enough to know they wouldn't listen to him anyway.

Before the sun set and inky darkness shrouded the stark landscape, they stripped all the horses, built a small fire in a depression where the light would be partially contained, and Agatha made a pot of coffee. Pieces of jerky were passed out. Fargo ate two and washed the meat down with several cups of the steaming coffee.

There was no moon. By the time he was ready to stand guard, Constance had fallen asleep, and Aggie was tucked under her blanket. He left the fire, where Sophia and Hugh were talking in low voices, and walked to the north end of the pass. A cool breeze fanned his face and rustled the pines below.

Fargo stood there for fifteen minutes or so, then turned and headed for the south end. A vague shape materialized out of the night on his left and he stopped.

"Here you are," Sophia said. "I picked the first stint so we could be together."

"Oh? What do you have in mind?"

Sophia ambled right up to him, set her rifle on the ground, and placed her hands on his broad shoulders. "What do you think, handsome?" she rejoined and planted her soft lips on his.

5

Fargo glanced toward the fire and saw that Hugh was flat on his back under a blanket. Agatha and Constance were both asleep. The horses were dozing or munching grass. He listened but heard nothing out of the ordinary. Satisfied they were safe for the time being, he allowed himself to respond to Sophia's advances, opening his mouth to entwine his tongue with hers. She let the kiss linger, rubbing against him all the while. When, at length, she pulled back, she wore a contented smile.

"Mmmmmm. That was nice. You do things to me, big man, that few men can." She ran her hand up and down his arm. "For a few seconds, though, you had me worried. You weren't heating up as you did last night."

Fargo nodded at her rifle. "Pick that up."

"How come?" Sophia asked, obeying. "Don't tell me you're not interested in having a little fun?"

He grabbed her wrist and hauled her to the stand of trees. Once screened from view, he leaned the Sharps against a trunk, then faced her and swooped both hands to her breasts.

Sophia gave a tiny gasp of delight and grinned. "I knew you really wanted me. A woman has a sixth sense about things like that."

"Do tell," Fargo said, locking his mouth on hers and reaching around to unfasten the buttons on the back of her dress. She looped her arms around his neck and rubbed her hips into him. His manhood surged, becoming iron hard, gouging into her pubic mound.

The dress parted like a peeled orange, and he pulled it down about her slim waist to gain access to her glorious globes. They were bigger than Agatha's, with longer, thicker nipples. He sucked on one, tweaking it with his tongue, and felt Sophia arch her spine.

"I'm already wet," she whispered throatily. "I've been thinking about you all day, Trailsman. Thinking about you doing me." She removed his hat, dropped it on the grass, and gripped his hair.

Fargo switched to her other breast. His mouth and hands combined aroused her to a fever pitch. She was squirming in lustful anticipation when he finally slid a hand between her thighs, and he heard her sharp intake of breath when he pressed his fingers against her slit. She wasn't fooling about being wet. Her underthings were drenched.

"Keep it up, honey," Sophia urged. "I can't wait to have you inside of me."

He was in no mood to rush. The old, familiar hunger was on him again, and he intended to feast fully on her womanly delights before satisfying her own carnal urges. Looping an arm around her waist, he slowly lowered her to the ground and lay beside her, their bodies flush.

"You probably won't believe this," Sophia said, "but it's been months since I had a man. Pa and his dumb idea about hiding in the damn mountains! He should have listened to Aggie and gone to a big city back east right off. Then we wouldn't be in this fix."

Fargo filed the information for future study. At the moment he was more interested in relieving the pleasant ache in his loins. He kissed and licked her neck, her shoulders, and her breasts. His mouth trailed a path down over her flat stomach until he could go no further because of her dress. Sliding over the folds of fabric, he poised above the junction of her smooth thighs and hiked the lower half of her dress up until the garment formed a bunched ring around her middle. The tantalizing aroma of her aroused womanhood tingled his nostrils as he nuzzled into her underthings. Then his right hand parted the material, and he was there, his nose in her crack. A flick of his tongue made her legs quiver uncontrollably.

"Oh, God," Sophia said softly so no one would overhear.

Fargo gave her nether region the same treatment he had given her upper, fastening his lips on her tiny throbbing knob and sucking to his heart's content. She shook and cooed and pushed on his head as if she was trying to force him into her body.

"Please, now!" she pleaded after a while. "Please!"

He gave her a taste of what she wanted. Inserting a forefinger into her slit, he felt her hot walls close around it like a glove. He began gently stroking her core to increase the fire boiling in her veins. She responded by moving her bottom in rhythm to his strokes.

"Ohhhhhhh, yes, honey!" Sophia breathed. "I'm in heaven."

Fargo continued stroking her until his own craving became irresistible. Rising on his knees, he lowered his pants, took his organ, and slowly inserted it into her slick sheath, inch by inch until he was all the way in. For a few seconds they both were still, relishing the sensation. Then he drew partway out and slammed into her with all the force he could muster.

Sophia came up off the ground and clung to him in rampant ecstasy. He pounded furiously, driving them both to the brink, until suddenly Sophia moaned and bit him on the shoulder, her inner walls contracting in sexual spasms. His temples were pulsing to the beat of his racing blood. Maintaining control was impossible. He exploded inside of her, his knees digging into the earth, his momentum lifting them both into the air. Time seemed to stand still as they panted in delirious fulfillment.

Gradually they coasted to a stop. Fargo lay on top of her, her warm skin against his. The exquisite sensation subsided. He turned his head to kiss her, then rolled to one side and gazed up at the stars dotting the firmament. Sophia giggled lightly. "What's so funny?" he whispered.

"Aggie. She'll have a hissy fit if she finds out we made love."

"She warned me to stay away from Connie and you."

"Did she now?" Sophia said. "Don't pay any attention to her, Skye. She's always been a selfish brat, ever since she was a kid. She has to get her own way all the time or she throws a fit. And where men are concerned, she thinks she can hog all the attractive ones for herself."

"Do you plan to tell her about this?"

"Not on your life. I'm not scared of her, mind you. But the last time we fought over a fella she about tore out my hair by the roots. I gave her a licking anyway, and she hasn't bothered me since." Sophia began adjusting her clothes. "I've learned to spare myself grief by keeping my mouth shut."

"Thanks. I wouldn't want her to stick a knife in my ribs when I wasn't looking," Fargo commented, only half joking.

"She might use a blade," Sophia said, pulling her dress over her shoulders. "Or she might get back at you through your food."

"How do you mean?"

Sophia glanced up and hesitated before answering. "Oh, she might put something in it to make you sick."

"Is that all?" Fargo asked casually, recalling the conversation about poison.

"Sure. What else?" Sophia rejoined. She made herself presentable, stood, and smoothed her dress. Her face was white against the dark, her features indistinct. "So which one of us is better?"

"What?"

"You heard me, lover. I know Aggie had you because she was bragging about it to Connie and me. Now that you've made love to the two of us, which one do you like the best?"

Fargo rose and tugged on his pants, stalling. No man in his right mind would ever answer such a question because no woman on earth liked to hear she was second-rate where lovemaking was concerned. He didn't trust Sophia not to do some bragging of her own if he told her she was better, and he didn't want Agatha angry at him.

"I'm waiting, handsome," Sophia said.

"I'd say you're both two of the best lovers I've ever known," Fargo fibbed, buckling his gun belt on. He deliberately avoided looking at her until his hat was firm on his head and he had the Sharps in his right hand.

Sophia was grinning. "You're a cagey one, Skye Fargo. And you know your way around women." She stepped close to kiss him on the cheek. "Any chance of you tagging along with us to St. Louis?"

"Afraid not. I'm not partial to big cities."

"Too bad," Sophia said, sighing. "We could have a grand time. I bet you'd look marvelous in a suit and a derby."

"I wouldn't be caught dead in an outfit like that."

She laughed and gave his shoulder a squeeze. "You never know. You might like city life if you give it half a chance. Think about my offer, and if you change your mind let me know. Just do it before we reach the plains."

"Why?"

"No special reason," Sophia said, grabbing her rifle and looking at the fire. "I could use a cup of coffee. How about you?"

"I'll stop for some in a minute," Fargo said, pondering her words as she moved off. Now what was this business about going with them to St. Louis? And why was it so important for him to decide before they were out of the mountains? He walked to the north side and scoured the slope below. Nothing stirred.

Hugh, Agatha, and Constance were all sleeping soundly when he returned to the fire. He gratefully took the tin cup Sophia handed him, and together they sat in silence and sipped at the strong brew. All of the horses, he noticed, were now asleep, even the Ovaro.

"I'm supposed to wake Aggie in a couple of hours," Sophia whispered, a twinkle in he eyes. "You'd better hide out in that stand of trees when it's her turn to help stand watch unless you're up to rolling in the hay again."

Fargo held the cup in both hands to warm his palms but made no comment. For someone who didn't want any grief, Sophia was remarkably careless. If Agatha wasn't asleep, if she was faking it, she now knew what Sophia and he had done.

"You remind me a lot of a man I met a couple of months back," Sophia mentioned absently. "He was a big man, like you, and he was tough as nails. His name was Harvey Stone. Ever heard of him?"

The name seared into Fargo's memory like a red-hot poker. Suddenly he knew where he had seen the Sharps with the brass tacks in the stock before. It had belonged to Stone, an army scout, a good man who had once saved a patrol he was guiding after they were surrounded by hostiles by dashing through the Indian lines and riding thirty miles in record time to the nearest fort for help. Fargo had played cards and drank with Stone on a half-dozen occasions. The last he'd heard, Stone was serving down in New Mexico Territory, which meant Murdock must have killed the scout there and taken the rifle.

"Something wrong?" Sophia inquired.

"No," Fargo said, hoping his face hadn't betrayed his thoughts. "I can't say as I've ever heard of this Stone. Why did you want to know?"

"He was a fine lover. The last one I had before you came along."

For two cents Fargo would have slugged her on the jaw. He glanced at Aggie, who tossed and mumbled something, then grasped the Hawken and straightened. "I'd better check the south end," he said.

"If you see that mountain lion, shoot it. Cougar meat is tastier than most. I could roast you some for breakfast and throw in a few biscuits."

He nodded and stepped away from the fire. "I know. I've eaten cougar a few times." He tried to piece together everything he had learned so far. Provided he was right about Murdock slaying Stone in New Mexico, then the whole Haddock gang must have been down there at the time. Why? Snake Haddock never went anywhere without a reason, and that reason always involved robbery. Maybe he was wrong about the gang hitting an army post.

A likelier idea gave him pause. What if the outlaws had struck a patrol, not a fort? Stone might have been serving as scout for the patrol and gone down when they did. But why would Haddock risk attacking the military? Soldiers rarely carried much money. They did sometimes escort wagons that transported large sums, however. Businessmen worried about the safety of shipping gold or silver often requested an army escort to ensure their precious cargo got to its destination intact.

It was all a guess, but it was the only guess that made perfect sense. And it might explain what was in the heavy wooden box, but not how Hugh Jennings came to have it in his possession.

Fargo gazed over his shoulder at the supplies stacked between the fire and the creek. Someone had spread a blanket on top, concealing the wooden box and everything else. Getting at it without drawing attention would be impossible. He must wait for a better chance.

A flat boulder on the crown of the south slope afforded

a place to sit and finish his coffee. He placed the rifle beside him and stared out over the darkness that stretched as far as the eye could see. Mountains, valleys, forest—all were shrouded in impenetrable gloom broken only by a tiny speck of flickering light far, far to the southwest. A campfire, he reasoned, twenty miles off or more.

He leaned on an elbow, drained the tin cup, and was putting it on the boulder when from the peak on his left came the rattle of small stones as they slid down from higher up. Instantly he was in a crouch, the Sharps ready for action. The peak reared hundreds of feet above him, a massive, windswept, spire of stone and dirt. No wildlife called it home, not even marmots or ground squirrels. There was no vegetation, not so much as a single weed. Yet something was up there.

Fargo moved to the edge of the boulder to better scan the peak. A hunch told him it might be the mountain lion. The big cats preferred high ground when prowling for prey since they could see deer and other animals from a long way off. Or the lion might have heard them approaching the pass earlier and sought shelter on the peak. Whatever the case, his main concern was that it didn't decide to come down and try for one of their horses.

The breeze picked up. Elsewhere a coyote yipped long and loud. A bird screeched. At the bottom of the mountain a bobcat snarled.

He held himself motionless, the rifle hammer cool under his thumb, his finger curled around the twin triggers. A scuffing noise from on high prompted him to cock the hammer, then pull the rear trigger to set the front trigger for firing. This was a unique feature of the Sharps, enabling the shooter to have a hair trigger for extremely accurate firing.

Skye's knees began to ache, but he disregarded the pain. Movement would enable the cougar to spot him if it didn't already know he was there. Mountain lions enjoyed exceptional eyesight, and like all cats they navigated rugged terrain with ease at night. He breathed shallowly, studying the peak and wishing the wind was blowing the other way so the horses could pick up the cougar's scent. A single whiff would have them upright and whinnying in fear, and he would know he was right.

How long he crouched he couldn't say, but after many minutes he decided there was no immediate threat and relaxed. Either the lion wasn't interested in the horses, it had left, or something else had made the sounds, perhaps merely rocks dislodged by the wind. He sat with his legs dangling over the side and glanced at the fire.

Agatha was awake. Sophia and she were huddled together, talking, and Aggie was gesturing angrily.

Now what were they up to?

Fargo remained where he was for another half an hour to be certain there was no danger, then he rose and carried the tin cup back. Sophia and Agatha were still nose to nose, whispering secretively. They stopped and looked up.

"More coffee?" Sophia asked.

"Not now, thanks," Fargo replied. He stared at Aggie. "Shouldn't you be resting while you have the chance?"

"I can't sleep."

"Just don't gripe tomorrow if you get tired and want to rest. We'll be pushing hard to put a lot of distance behind us."

Agatha grinned, scrunched up her nose, then stuck out her tongue. "Don't fret none over me, big man. I can hold my own. If I was you, I'd be more concerned about myself. It's a long way to the prairie and a lot of things can happen along the way. You watch out for your own hide."

"I always do," Fargo said, wondering if that was her way of making a subtle threat. He headed for the north side of the pass, annoyed at himself for ever taking up with the family. It had seemed like the right thing to do at the time, but now he had half a mind to ride off and leave them to Snake Haddock. Then he thought of Harvey Stone and that mysterious wooden box and decided he would see it through to the end, come what may.

The hours passed uneventfully. Aggie relieved Sophia, who turned in, but strangely Aggie said little to Fargo, and she made a point of going off by herself a lot to patrol the perimeter. He'd expected a repeat of her performance in the ravine and was puzzled by her newfound self-control. He couldn't shake the nagging feeling that the family was up to something. Agatha, in particular, was the one to keep an eye on. She was like that coral snake he had come across in Florida a while back—pretty and graceful outside but as deadly as could be inside.

Fargo was glad when Hugh relieved him. The long day had left him greatly fatigued. He arranged his bedroll near the string of horses to be close to the Ovaro. Should anyone approach too near, even one of the Jennings clan, the stallion would let him know. Lying on his back, he propped his head in his palms and gazed at the heavens until sleep claimed him.

Dawn brought a flurry of activity. Agatha made breakfast while the rest of her family loaded their supplies on the packhorses. Fargo was watering the pinto at the time. He saw them carry the wooden box over and made a point of noticing which horse was picked to do the honors. Hugh didn't pick the same animal he had yesterday, which indicated to Fargo that the box was so heavy it was necessary to switch horses in order to give the one that bore it yesterday a break. Somehow or other he must get a closer look at the box, and today might be the day.

After flapjacks and coffee they mounted up. Fargo assumed the lead as usual. He rode out the south end of the pass and down toward the virgin forest at the bottom of the mountain. A golden crown rimmed the eastern horizon. The air was crisp and clear, as it always was at that altitude. A pair of ravens flapped by overhead, the swish of their wings surprisingly loud in the rarefied atmosphere.

He scanned the landscape but saw no sign of smoke. War parties, however, often made cold camps, so the absence of smoke didn't mean he could let his guard down. The creek meandered on their right; a boulder strewn area was on their left. An early rising marmot took one look at them, whistled its shrill alarm, and raced for its burrow among the boulders.

Fargo heard the clomp of hoofs as Constance rode up to join him.

"Mind if we chat a spell, Mr. Fargo? You've spent a lot of time with my sisters but not much with me, and I'd like to get to know you better."

He glanced at her. Connie was the youngest but the hardest to read because her features rarely gave away her inner feelings. Unlike Aggie and Sophia, both of whom were full-blooded firebrands who let their emotions rule their lives, Constance was reserved, almost aloof, as different from her lusty sisters as night from day. "What do you want to talk about?"

"Oh, I don't know. Anything," Connie said. "I get godawful tired of listening to my older sisters talk about their escapades with men. That's practically all they care about, you see." Her mouth curled upward. "But then, from what I hear, you already know that."

"What have you heard?"

"Oh, a little of this, a little of that."

"Does it upset you?"

Connie looked at him. "Not at all. I admire a man who knows what he wants and goes after it with both barrels." She snickered. "Besides, you're hardly a monk. And it would take a monk to be able to resist the charms my sisters have to offer."

Fargo smiled. "You know your sisters well."

The humor left Connie's eyes. "All too well, I'm afraid. You'd do well not to take them lightly, Mr. Fargo. Nor my pa. Many who have ended up regretting it. A lot of good people have . . ." She caught herself and quickly averted her face.

"Have what?"

"Have learned the hard way that my family isn't like most. My pa is an outlaw, my ma was a common whore, and most of us are no better."

Fargo glanced over his shoulder. The others were far enough back that they couldn't overhear. "If you feel this way," he said, "why do you stick with them?"

"Where would I go? What would I do? I have no skills. And we both know what can happen to a lone woman wandering around the West."

"You could always go back east."

"No, I couldn't. City life isn't for me." She motioned at the sweeping vista below. "This is the kind of country I like, and western folks are my kind of people. Friendly, decent folks who would give you the shirt off their backs if you were in need." She paused. "Well, almost all western folks are that way. Then there are sons of bitches like Snake Haddock and my dear pa."

Fargo didn't know what to say. He'd had no idea Connie felt this way, and he wondered why she was confiding in him when they hardly knew each other. About to ask her, he stiffened when a shrill shriek erupted from the rear.

"Indians! Up there!" Sophia cried, pointing at the pass.

He saw them, four warriors on war ponies framed between the twin peaks, a moment before the braves started down the slope.

6

Hugh Jennings, who was at the end of the line, twisted, whipped out his rifle, and raised it to his shoulder.

"No!" Fargo shouted, wheeling the Ovaro and jabbing his spurs into its flanks. "Don't shoot!" The four Indians—Bloods by their style of dress and the way they wore their long hair—had made no move to use their weapons. Two were armed with bows, two with lances. They approached warily, the tallest warrior out in front.

"Why the hell not?" Hugh snapped as Fargo came up. "They'll take our hair if we give them half a chance."

"Maybe not," Fargo said. Bloods were notorious for killing whites, but they weren't as bloodthirsty as the Blackfeet. That was because the Bloods were reluctant to attack unless they outnumbered their enemies or they could spring an ambush without fear of being caught. They were proud and warlike, but innately cautious. They weren't prone to taking risks as were the Blackfeet, perhaps because there were fewer of them and they could ill afford to lose a single man. He knew of instances when parties of whites had passed safely through their territory in exchange for guns, blankets, or trinkets.

The four Indians reined up a dozen feet off, and the tall one used sign language to say, "We have come in peace. I am Stalking Wolf of the Bloods. We would have words with you."

Fargo moved in front of Hugh to prevent the hothead from firing, draped his reins over the pommel, and responded in sign. "We are listening."

Stalking Wolf gazed past Fargo at Agatha and Sophia. "We have been following you since you left the cliff, and we have seen that you have many guns and blankets. You have more than you need."

"What's the buck sayin'?" Hugh interrupted. "Why was he lookin' at my girls?"

"Keep quiet," Fargo replied. "We might be able to get out of this without bloodshed if you don't make trouble."

"Fine with me. But if that bastard gives my girls the eye again, I aim to cut loose. Hell, I can probably plug all four of these savages before they get off an arrow."

"And what if there are more up in the boulders or down in the trees?"

There was a pause.

"Damn. I didn't think of that. Go on. Do what you have to."

The Bloods had listened to the exchange with interest although it was doubtful any of them spoke English. Stalking Wolf waited until Hugh stopped speaking, then employed sign language again, "I do not like that man."

"We have something in common," Fargo responded.

"Are you the leader or is he?"

"I am."

Stalking Wolf pondered a few moments. Then he motioned at his companions. "This land is ours, white man. We know every rock, every blade of grass."

Fargo knew what was coming and sat quietly.

"For more winters than a man can count we roamed as we pleased and did as we liked. We fought so well that the Blackfeet chose us as allies. Other tribes know of our strength and fear the Bloods."

For a warrior Stalking Wolf was long-winded. Fargo rested his right hand on his thigh, close to his Colt, and surveyed the boulders. If there were more warriors lurking in ambush, that was where they would be.

"Until the whites came to our land, all was well. But they came and killed almost all of the beaver and many of the buffalo, and they did not even think to ask us if they could do this. When we visited them they acted as if we were less than they, and some of our people were killed. Since then we have warred on the whites."

Fargo's countenance hardened. "If you want a fight you came to the right person."

"Hard talk is not needed. If we wanted to kill you, all of you would already be dead," Stalking Wolf signed. "But we have decided to let you live and travel through our land as you see fit."

"We are grateful."

"I am not done. We will let you go in peace, we will let you share the bounty the land has to offer, if you will share the things *you* have with *us*."

Fargo could have said no. Most whites would have. And if the Bloods forced the issue he could, as Hugh had wanted to do, slay all four before they touched their weapons. None of them—not the Bloods, not Hugh or his daughters—knew how fast he was on the draw. But he had lived among Indians and knew their ways. He knew that what Stalking Wolf had said was true. Most of the bad feelings between whites and redskins was the fault of the former. Few white men ever bothered to make honest attempts to understand the Indian. The majority, in fact, looked down their noses at a race they considered heathen and inferior. "Your offer is fair," he signed. "What would you have us give you?"

"Three rifles, two revolvers, four blankets, and one of your pack animals."

"We will give you two blankets," Fargo said.

"You insult us, white man. We will accept two rifles, two blankets, and your pack horse. Nothing less."

Despite the stern tone Stalking Wolf used, Fargo had dealt with too many Indians from various tribes to be fooled into thinking the warrior was really angry. Indians had bartering down to a fine science, and negotiations sometimes went on for days when tribes met to settle disputes. "Two blankets, flour, sugar, and three tin cups," he signed. "That is our final offer."

Stalking Wolf adopted an appropriately indignant look. "Our wives would like the blankets, flour, sugar, and cups, but what of us? We are men."

Fargo had a choice to make. He wasn't partial to giving guns to warriors who might later use the weapons against innocent pilgrims heading west, but he was certain the Bloods would not let his party leave in peace without receiving at least one gun as a token gesture of good will. "We do not have two rifles to spare, but I do have a fine rifle I can give you in friendship if the others are willing to go without one."

He was taking a calculated gamble. From prior dealings with Indians, he knew that the way to get on their good side was to single out a chief or other leader and make friends with him. The chief would then keep the rest in line. Stalking Wolf was the apparent head of this war party, so if he made Stalking Wolf happy, the rest would have to go along or risk angering him.

"Is this rifle the same kind as was traded to my people by the fur companies?—guns that shoot short distances and sometimes blow up in the faces of the shooters?"

"No," Fargo signed, well aware of the cheap guns greedy traders had swapped for bundles of prime pelts. He reached behind him and pulled Stone's rifle free of the bedroll, then held it out for the Bloods to see. Since there was no word in sign language for a Sharps, he lowered the rifle and improvised. "This is a fine gun, just like my own. In our tongue it is called a Shoots-Far gun. If you want it, I will also give you a bag of ammunition."

The tall warrior tried not to let his keen interest show, but he could scarcely contain himself as he came forward several yards to better study the Sharps.

Fargo rested the rifle on his thighs and signed, "Would you like to hold it?"

Stalking Wolf responded eagerly.

"What do you think you're doing, Trailsman?" Hugh Jennings demanded.

"Making a deal so we can ride off without a fight."

"You're handing over that Sharps?"

Fargo nodded.

"Like hell you are," Hugh said, and suddenly leaned to the left to give himself a clear shot at the same instant he leveled his rifle and fired from the waist.

It was so unexpected and happened so swiftly that there was nothing Fargo could do. He twisted and saw Stalking Wolf tumbling to the ground, a crimson hole in the warrior's chest. The three other Bloods were momentarily transfixed by the sight, too stunned to try to bring their weapons to bear. A second later they did just that, but by then Hugh had unlimbered his revolver and fired, hitting one of the braves in the temple.

The last two Bloods finally galvanized into action. There was no reasoning with them now, no other recourse but for Fargo to defend himself or be killed by the enraged warriors. Venting a curse, he drew the Colt and sent a slug into a warrior notching an arrow to a bowstring. His second shot caught the last Blood as the man threw back his arm to hurl a lance. Both men hit the earth at the same time.

"There," Hugh said in satisfaction. "Now they don't get their greasy hands on that rifle."

Furious, his face livid, Fargo twisted and pointed the Colt at Hugh. For a heartbeat he came close to squeezing the trigger. He felt an almost overwhelming urge to riddle the old bastard with bullets, and his arm trembled from the intensity of his emotion.

Hugh gaped and recoiled, his own revolver and rifle angled downward, fear blossoming as he realized he was staring death in the face. He blanched, gulped, and forced a wan grin. "What's gotten your goat, Fargo? Don't tell me you give a damn about a bunch of mangy Injuns?"

"You didn't have to kill them," Fargo growled, struggling to regain his composure. He saw Agatha and Sophia gawking in stunned disbelief. Constance, however, appeared sad.

"Haven't you heard? The only good Injun is a dead one," Hugh stated. He cocked his head, his brow knitting. "Hell, man. You know this bunch would have killed us if they thought they could get away with it. I really don't see why you're so upset."

Fargo's fury evaporated, and he shoved the Colt into his holster. Killing Hugh would be a waste of lead. The man's attitude toward Indians was no different from that of the majority of whites. And if he shot Hugh, the women would be left to fend for themselves unless he was willing to go to the trouble of escorting them to the nearest fort. "I've lived among Indians," he said flatly and shoved the spare Sharps back into his bedroll.

"We're heading out," he announced curtly and goaded the Ovaro down the slope past the women until he was in the lead once more. He was worried that there might be more Bloods in the area who would come to investigate the shots. They had to push on and keep an eye on their back trail.

The dense forest closed around them, and he struck off to the southeast. An oppressive atmosphere seemed to envelop the woodland, due to the branches screening out much of the sunlight and casting the forest in an eerie twilight. Low limbs often snatched at their clothes or compelled them to duck low to pass underneath. A thick carpet of dead pine needles muffled the hoof beats of their mounts, and other than the dull drumming there was no sound. The gunshots had silenced the wildlife.

Fargo came to a narrow creek and rode into it, then turned to the left and followed it for half a mile. The ploy might throw off pursuers although a seasoned tracker would catch onto the trick in no time. He left the water and entered a winding valley rimmed by towering snow-crowned peaks. A glance showed the Jennings family were strung out in a line, Agatha at the rear with her rifle in hand.

Connie dug her heels into her horse and joined him. "Mind a little company?"

"Why should I mind?" Fargo rejoined, scouring the mountains and the valley ahead.

"You have the look of a rabid wolf about to snap someone's head off," Connie said. "Not that I blame you. For what it's worth, I'm sorry about what happened back there. I should have warned you that my pa hates Injuns. A friend of his was killed by Comanches when he was a boy."

Fargo spied a solitary red hawk spiraling above the aspen on a mountain to the right. It made him think of how nice it would be to be on his own again without a care in the world. When would he learn not to meddle in the affairs of others?

"My sisters are the same way," Constance continued. "Pa has filled them with hate for every redskin that lives. Aggie once shot an old toothless Arapaho who came to our camp one evening to beg for food."

"I'm not surprised to hear it," Fargo said, glancing at her. "And you? How do you feel about Indians?"

Connie shrugged. "I don't bear hate toward anyone. All I want is to have a normal life like most other folks, to find a decent man, settle down, and raise five or six pesky kids." She smiled wistfully. "Is that too much to ask of life?"

"What's stopping you?"

"My family."

"You're a grown woman. You can do as you please."

"I wish it was that simple," Connie said, frowning.

"My ma was big on family life, even though Pa was gone most of the time. She never minded having to raise us pretty much by her lonesome. She always told us that we should stick together through thick and thin, that the only people in the whole world we could trust completely was each other. And for all Pa's faults, he feels the same way about family." She sighed. "I can't leave them, Fargo. I feel guilty just thinking about doing it."

"So you'll be miserable the rest of your life?"

"It's that obvious?" Connie asked, then answered her own question. "Yes, I suppose it is. I've always been different from my sisters, even when we were young. All they were ever interested in was boys and raising hell. Sophia likes to joke that maybe I had a different pa than Aggie and her, and maybe she's right."

"I don't make a habit of giving advice unless someone asks for it," Fargo said, "but you had better face facts or you'll never know the happiness you want. Your family is a pack of sidewinders. Unless you get shy of them, your whole life will be ruined."

"I can't," Connie said plaintively.

"It's your life," Fargo stressed.

They reached the end of the verdant valley where a large beaver dam had formed a wide pond. He called a halt and took the stallion to the water's edge to let it drink. Hugh, Agatha, and Sophia were clustered by the pack animals, talking in low tones. What were they plotting? he mused and turned as Connie brought her horse over.

"How soon before we reach the plains?" she asked.

"If we can keep this pace, tomorrow afternoon at the latest," Fargo answered.

"You should leave us before then."

"Why? Don't you like my company?" Fargo joked.

"I like you a lot," Connie said frankly. "Which is why I'm advising you to cut out well before we get to the prairie. Don't worry. We'll manage on our own."

"I'm at the point where I don't give a damn what happens to the rest of your family," Fargo declared, "but I do care what happens to you. Why not let me take you to a town or a military post where you can get a stage to anywhere you want to go?"

Connie squatted and dipped a hand in the pond, then

cooled her cheeks and neck. "I'm tempted, Skye," she said softly. "I truly am." She bowed her head. "Tell you what. I'll think it over and let you know tomorrow morning. All right?"

"Fine," Fargo said, pleased he might be able to help her salvage her life before Hugh and the other two dragged her down with them. She was the only nice one in the bunch. He suddenly decided to take advantage of her friendliness and asked, "What's in the wooden box, Connie?"

She straightened, fright lining her lovely features, and cast an anxious glance at her family. Then she stepped close to him and whispered, "If you want to live, don't mention that box again! Don't even look at it if you see them unloading it from the packhorse."

"How did you come by it?"

"Aren't you listening to me?" Connie snapped, her voice rising. She clenched her fists and made a visible effort to control herself. "If they suspect you're interested in that box, they'll kill you."

"I can take care of myself," Fargo said.

"Could you shoot Aggie or Sophia? Because if you're not careful, that's what you'll have to do." She gripped his wrist. "Please, Skye! Don't make an issue of this. Just do as I say and cut out—"

"Is something wrong, girl?"

Fargo hadn't noticed Hugh approach. He felt Connie's nails gouge into his skin, then she let go and turned.

"No, Pa. Nothing is wrong."

Hugh's eyes narrowed as he coldly regarded Fargo. "Then why were you actin' so upset a few seconds ago? It looked to me as if the two of you was havin' an argument."

"We weren't, Pa."

"Is he treatin' you proper?"

Fargo came to her rescue by moving between them and placing his hands on his hips. "I take that as an insult, Jennings," he declared. His voice lowered to a snarl. "And I don't like being insulted."

Like a cornered rodent, Hugh blinked and backed up a step, his thin lips twitching, the fingers of his gun hand flexing and unflexing. "A man has a right to watch out for his own," he said defensively. "For all I know, you said something to upset her."

"He didn't, Pa," Connie said.

"You heard her," Fargo said.

"All right. Calm down," Hugh responded, his gun hand relaxing. "I guess I was wrong." He began to turn, then looked at Fargo. "But I'll be honest with you, mister. I don't think as highly of you as I first did. Once we reach the plains, I want you to leave us."

"I'll leave now if you want," Fargo angrily replied, and could have kicked himself for being so rash. He wanted to tag along with them until Connie made up her mind whether she was leaving or staying.

Hugh hesitated. Clearly, he was tempted to tell Fargo to go, but he shook his head and said, "A few bad words shouldn't spoil everything. I'd be obliged if you'll ride with us until we're out of these mountains, and I promise to behave myself from here on out."

The outlaw wasn't fooling Fargo. The only reason Hugh wanted him along was in case the Haddock gang caught up with them. "I said I'd guide you, and I will," Fargo said.

"Thanks," Hugh said without a hint of genuine warmth. He walked back to Aggie and Sophia.

Connie also started to walk off, but paused. "I'm sorry you're involved in this, Skye. You're only trying to help us. Just like the others." Her shoulders slumped, she moved toward her family.

What others? Fargo was no closer to learning the secret of the wooden box, but he was more determined than ever to learn what was inside. The contents might help unravel the fate of Harvey Stone. Since he would have only one more night alone with the Jennings family, he must wait until most of them were asleep and somehow get it open. He now understood why Hugh had insisted on sharing guard duty with the women; there would always be one of the family awake to keep an eye on their precious box.

"Time to go," he said and mounted. Riding with his back to a man like Hugh Jennings made him uneasy, but he doubted Hugh would try anything until sometime tomorrow. When Hugh was convinced Snake Haddock couldn't find them, then Hugh would show his true colors.

Fargo skirted a mountain covered with pines, crossed a hill so he could survey their back trail from the top, and rode into a green valley where there was evidence an Indian tribe had camped within the past week. A dozen black areas marked the charred embers from lodge fires. There were circular impressions where the lodges had stood, and the ground bore hundreds of hoof prints. A broken arrow and a torn, discarded parfleche revealed the tribe had been Shoshonis. Few Indians were friendlier to whites. The tribe had trekked westward after breaking camp.

"Blackfeet or Bloods?" Hugh called out.

"Neither," Fargo said and told him.

"Then we must be well clear of Blackfoot country," Hugh commented. "The Shoshonis wouldn't go anywhere near it." He chuckled. "Yep. We're makin' real good time."

Fargo pressed on. Miles farther, when he looked over his shoulder, he saw Agatha and Hugh in an angry discussion but thought little of it. Shortly afterward, Aggie rode up to be beside Connie.

Before them loomed a series of jagged mountains, the last great barrier between them and the foothills. Fargo knew of a pass that would shave hours off their traveling time. To reach it, they had to climb a winding game trail that curved back and forth up the slope of a barren mountain, a trail long used by mountain sheep, deer, and occasional elk, but rarely by humans. At points the trail was barely wide enough for their horses to walk. Every so often, where it curved, there was enough room for their mounts to turn around if need be, and it was when they were two thirds of the way up that Fargo reached just such a shelf and reined up close to the edge to scan the countryside. He heard a horse come onto the shelf, then Aggie's soft voice.

"Fargo?"

"What?" The Trailsman responded, shifting in the saddle to gaze at her. Too late, he saw the rifle streaking at his head as she swung it like a club. He felt a jarring impact when the stock connected with his forehead, the brutal jolt knocking him off the Ovaro, and the last sensation he experienced was the rush of air past his face as he plummeted over the side.

7

Dimly Skye Fargo became aware of a rocking motion, as if he was adrift on the ocean and was being buffeted by rolling waves. Next he felt pain, incredibly intense pain, from ear to ear. A sticky substance coated part of his face. He heard voices, but they seemed to be coming from the far end of a long tunnel. Then he became aware of something pressing on his chest, and he opened his eyes. Or tried to. Only the right eye would open, and for a few moments he couldn't make sense of what he saw. Ringing him were four rough characters. One, a burly man whose right cheek bore a jagged scar, had his foot on Fargo's chest and was shaking him. "Stop it," Fargo rasped out, barely able to speak, his throat as dry as a desert.

"Well, I'll be damned, boys," the man with the scar declared. "This hombre is alive after all." He turned and cupped a hand to his mouth. "Snake! He's come around. What do you want us to do with him?"

Fargo fought off a fleeting urge to panic. The men surrounding him were part of Snake Haddock's gang! He tried to push himself up, but he was too weak.

"I say we put this fella out of his misery and divide up his duds," commented one of the foursome. "He ain't going to live anyhow."

"He does look poorly," said another, who craned his neck to stare upward. "Must of fallen quite a ways."

"I wonder what happened?" said the third.

"Maybe his horse throwed him," said the man with the scar.

Fargo heard heavy boot steps and saw the quartet step back. Suddenly a huge man appeared, a bear of a brute well over six feet tall and weighing two hundred and fifty pounds or more. He had a bushy black beard and a bulbous nose. His clothes were homespun, faded and worn from much use. A black hat crowned his square head. Most remarkable were his penetrating green eyes, eyes that raked over Fargo, then settled on Fargo's face.

"The name is Haddock, mister. Who are you?"

"Fargo," he croaked, and licked his parched lips. Why was he so dry, so thirsty?

"We're looking for a man and three women who go by the handle of Jennings. You wouldn't happen to have seen them, would you?"

Fargo's mind worked furiously. Wolney must have described him to Haddock, must have told Snake all about the part he played in thwarting their plans to hold the Jennings family prisoner until the outlaw leader arrived at the cliff. So Haddock must be toying with him, and here he was helpless, completely at the gang's mercy. His only hope lay in talking his way out of the fix Agatha had put him in. "Yeah, I know them," he answered. "Who do you think did this to me?"

"Interesting," Haddock said, crouching. He glanced at the man bearing the scar. "Porter, get me a canteen and something to clean this blood off with."

"Right away, boss," Porter said, and hastened away.

Snake Haddock leaned down to examine Fargo's head. "You've got a nasty gash and you've lost a lot of blood. How exactly did this happen?" he inquired.

"Agatha Jennings hit me with a rifle," Fargo detailed and was flabbergasted when Haddock threw back his bull head and roared with laughter. Some of the other men joined in.

"That sure enough sounds like our Aggie," Haddock said. "She's a hellcat when she's riled. What did you do to get her mad at you?"

"Nothing that I can think of," Fargo said, expecting Wolney to appear at any moment. "I'd agreed to serve as their guide." He felt his strength slowly returning and lifted his right hand. "I sure as hell never expected this to happen."

"Did Aggie screw you?"

Fargo froze with his hand halfway to his face.

"No need to deny it if it's true," Haddock said with a smirk. "Aggie screws everything wearing pants. If she could, I'd swear that gal would bed every man in this country." He nodded at the three men standing nearby. "Hell, she's had all of them two or three times. Me, I was always partial to Sophia." His eyes became flinty. "Did you screw her, too?"

"No," Fargo lied.

Haddock pursed his lips. "How did you happen to hook up with old Hugh and his girls?"

Fargo didn't quite know what to make of the way the outlaw was acting. He was confused. Why was Haddock being so damn polite if the man knew or guessed that he was the one who had killed Murdock and two other members of Haddock's gang? He grimaced and made a show of being in greater pain than he was so he could stall, and tilted his head. Fifteen yards off were five men on horseback and the horses that belonged to Haddock, Porter, and the three hard cases near at hand. Wolney was nowhere to be seen. "I just ran into them a couple of days ago," he answered.

"Did you happen to see any sign of three men? They ride with me, and they were supposed to track Hugh down. One is named Murdock."

"Can't say as I did."

Porter returned bearing a canteen and a strip of dirty cloth. "This was all I could find," he said, waving the cloth. "I use it to clean my guns."

"It'll do," Haddock said, taking both and setting them on Fargo's chest. "Here. Pull yourself together while the boys and me decide what to do with you." He reached out and plucked Fargo's Colt from its holster. "I'll hold onto this for you for a spell. There are men who would die for the chance to plug me, and I don't cotton to the notion of taking lead in the back." Standing, Haddock motioned for the others to join him as he moved toward the horses.

It took every bit of resolve Fargo could muster to enable him to sit up. He was appalled by his weakness. Opening the canteen, he poured water onto the cloth, then applied the cloth to his face, rubbing hard, removing the caked blood. He worked carefully around his left eye, loosening the eyelid, until it parted and he could see out of both eyes again. His hat was lying to his left. He raised his hand and gingerly felt along his scalp and through his hair. The gash Haddock had mentioned was several inches above his right ear. Just touching it produced a lancing pang that set his temples to pounding.

Fargo slowly got to his knees. He gazed up at the mountain, shocked to see he had fallen two hundred feet. Not far off was a boulder with a splash of crimson down the middle. Now he knew how he had acquired the gash. He must have bounced off it on the way down. The Jennings clan, of course, were long gone, and so was the Ovaro. Scowling, he peered at the sky and was amazed to see the sun only a few hours above the eastern horizon. That explained why he was so thirsty. He had been unconscious for eighteen hours.

He took a long swig from the canteen, then another, relishing the feel of the cool water as it soothed his throat. He would have polished off every last drop, but Snake Haddock strolled back with his men in tow.

"You say you were acting as guide for Hugh and those tomcats of his. Where were you taking them?"

Fargo told the truth. A lie would do no good since Haddock had undoubtedly guessed the Jennings family were making for the plains by the direction the tracks were leading. "They wanted me to take them to the prairie. Hugh claimed he didn't know his way around this territory very well."

"Hmmmm," was all Haddock said. He turned to Porter. "Mount up. Tell Jessup I want him to ride double with Fargo here for a while. When his horse tires, someone else will take over."

"I'm grateful for the help," Fargo said.

"Don't thank me yet, mister. I'm taking you along to get to the bottom of this. And if I find you've lied, I'll peel off your skin with my butcher knife and stake you out for the buzzards." Haddock jerked his thumb at two of his men. "Put him on Jessup's horse."

Fargo was helpless to resist as the pair seized him by the arms. Porter took the canteen and cloth, then jammed his hat on his head, making him flinch. They hauled him to the horses. He tried to stand and got his feet under him just as they halted beside a bay. The skinny outlaw in the saddle grinned.

"So I'm to take you, am I? I'm Bo Jessup, stranger." He patted the revolver on his right hip. "Some folks say

I'm right handy with this, so don't get any notions about dumping me and trying to run off. I'll put three bullets into you before you get ten feet."

The two men holding Fargo each heaved, and he found himself perched behind Bo Jessup. Dizziness caused him to sway, and he reached for the cantle for support. Haddock and the rest mounted. At a gesture from Snake they all moved out, heading up the same narrow game trail Fargo had climbed the day before. A swarthy man in a high-crowned brown hat assumed the lead, and from the way he often bent down to closely study the ground it was apparent he was a first-rate tracker.

Fargo concentrated on holding on and staying upright. His head ached with every stride Jessup's horse took. He tucked his chin low, closed his eyes, and waited for the climb to end.

Jessup, it turned out, was the talkative sort. "I didn't catch your name, mister?"

"Fargo."

"Have we ever met?"

Fargo opened his eyes. "No."

"Are you sure? Something about your name is familiar. I've been all over the West from north to south and east to west. Maybe we've crossed paths somewhere."

"I don't think so," Fargo said.

"It'll come to me," Jessup predicted. "I never forget a name or a face. If I've heard of you, I'll remember where."

As if Fargo didn't have enough to worry about. He had deliberately told them only his last name in the hope he wouldn't be recognized. If Haddock found out who he was, the outlaw might kill him out of sheer spite. It was well known that the Trailsman had no fondness for those who lived outside the law.

"Are you by any chance on the dodge?" Jessup asked.

"No."

"Too bad. We can use a good man. We lost four in the past week alone. Three up and disappeared without a trace, and the fourth got himself killed by four Indians. We found their tracks, but we couldn't tell if they were Blackfeet or Bloods." Jessup shuddered. "Wolney was his name, and you should have seen him when those savages got done having their fun. They hung him upside down over a fire and roasted him good and proper. He looked just like a slab of burnt beef."

Fargo realized the same Bloods who had tried to barter for weapons were the same ones who must have killed Wolney. Stalking Wolf and those three braves had inadvertently done him a favor by preventing the hard case from reporting to Haddock. They must have backtracked Wolney to the vicinity of the cliff and then found the Jennings family.

Now he understood why Haddock hadn't slain him on the spot. The outlaws had no idea he had shot three of their own. But Haddock was suspicious of his claim that he had only served as the Jennings's guide.

"You could do worse than ride with us," Jessup was saying. "We're the meanest bunch of long riders north of the Pecos and damn proud of it. Do you know who our boss is?" Jessup unexpectedly asked.

"Yep," Fargo admitted. He had never met an outlaw so proud of his calling before. Was that why Jessup was so intent on having him join them?

Jessup nodded. "Most folks have heard of Snake Haddock. He's killed more men and stolen more money than anyone in history. I've been with him seven years, and I've yet to get a scratch." He glanced back and beamed. "Snake is my brother-in-law."

They eventually reached the top of the mountain and negotiated the winding pass. Foothills covered with pristine forest unfolded before them. Once down the slope, the outlaws rode swiftly. Snake Haddock was obviously in a hurry to overtake the Jennings.

Fargo held on tight and wished his headache would go away. Several times he considered making a grab for Jessup's gun and trying to escape. In his condition, though, he wouldn't get far. It was better, he decided, to wait until he felt stronger, then made his bid for freedom.

Snake Haddock and his men were all superb horsemen. Years of living on the run had made them the equal of Comanches. They rode effortlessly, horses and riders as one. An hour out from the mountain they found where Hugh Jennings and his daughters had camped the previous night. While the rest stayed in their saddles, the tracker in the brown hat got down to inspect the ground.

"One of them is still riding Murdock's dun," the man reported. "They slept in late this morning. Didn't leave until two hours ago. Hugh must figure he's lost us."

"He'll learn the hard way not to double-cross me," Haddock said. "Let's go. If we push our horses we should catch that son of a bitch about noontime."

The mention of Murdock's dun jarred Fargo's memory. They had left Murdock lying at the base of the cliff. Haddock should have found him. Yet none of the outlaws knew Murdock was dead. Had the Bloods done something with the body? Perhaps taken it into the trees where they could scalp it undisturbed? Or had that mountain lion found it and dragged it off to eat?

For two hours the outlaw band rode hellbent for leather. Jessup, his animal burdened with extra weight, brought up the rear. Porter and another man hung back, always keeping an eye on Fargo, making no secret of their intentions.

The tracker reached the top of a hill and abruptly reined up. The rest followed suit. A mile off was the reason, a plume of white smoke spiraling skyward.

"It's them," the tracker said. "They've stopped to rest."

"Their mistake," Snake stated. "Burnett, go check it out. We'll wait right here."

With a flick of his reins the tracker took off down the hill and into the trees.

Haddock looked at Fargo. "Burnett is one of the best trackers I've ever met. He told us there was someone new riding with Hugh back at the cliff, where we found Hugh's dead horse." He pushed his hat back. "I plumb forgot to ask you. Who shot that animal?"

"I don't know. It was already dead when I found Hugh and his daughters."

"Was it indeed?" Snake said, and snorted. "Mister, you must take me for the biggest fool who ever lived. In a short while I'm going to teach you how wrong you are."

"So much for you joining us," Bo Jessup said and laughed.

Fargo saw nothing humorous in his predicament. He had regained much of his strength and his headache wasn't quite as bad, but he was in no shape to take on ten hardened killers. His only ace in the hole was the Arkansas toothpick, snug in his right boot.

"What about those hellcats, Snake?" Porter asked. "Are we going to let them live?"

"I haven't made up my mind yet," Haddock said.

"They might not have had anything to do with it. Hugh may have cooked up the whole scheme."

"Maybe, but knowing Aggie the way I do, I'd bet she was the brains behind it. Old Hugh should have known better than to listen to her. That woman has more greed in her little finger than most people do in their whole body." Haddock grinned. "And I should know. I'm an expert on it."

"I never figured Hugh could be so dumb," commented one of the other outlaws. "He must have known we'd hunt him down."

"He didn't count on us finding out so soon," Bo Jessup threw in. "And we wouldn't have, too, if Snake hadn't become a mite suspicious."

"What do you have planned for Hugh, Snake?" inquired another rider.

"You'll see," Snake said. "And you won't ever forget it."

On that ominous note they fell silent. Fargo realized he might well share Hugh's fate if Haddock found out he was the one who killed Murdock and those other two. If he was smart, he would make his break before the outlaws reached the Jennings's camp. Every minute thereafter increased the odds he would be dead by dark.

His stomach grumbled, reminding him he hadn't eaten since the morning before. And his mouth was still terribly dry. He nudged Jessup. "I could use some water."

"Could you now?" the outlaw responded sarcastically. "Well, you're welcome to lick the sweat off my horse any time you want. If that's not enough, I'm sure my pards will let you lick their horses."

They all thought that was hilarious.

Soon Burnett returned and reined up in front of Haddock. "I was right, Snake. It's them. They made camp on the west side of a pond. Connie is fixing grub. Her sisters are in the water, taking a bath."

"And Hugh?"

"He was drinking coffee by the fire when I left."

"The box?"

"Hugh has it right beside him."

"Then let's go invite ourselves to dinner, boys," Snake said, goading his horse into motion.

Once more Jessup rode at the back of the bunch. And once more Porter and another outlaw stayed close to prevent Fargo from trying anything.

Fargo was sorely tempted to try anyway. He eased his right hand forward, toward Jessup's revolver, sliding it along his leg so none of the outlaws would notice. But one of them had eyes like an eagle.

"I wouldn't try that if I was you, mister," Porter said, his own hand on the butt of his six-shooter. "Not unless you're in a hurry to die."

Thwarted, Fargo resigned himself to make the best of whatever happened next. The outlaws slowed, then held their mounts to a walk as they approached the pond. They heard light laughter. Through the trees they could see Agatha and Sophia standing in waist-deep water, splashing each other, their wet breasts glistening in the sunlight. Constance and Hugh were talking at the fire.

Haddock gestured, and his men promptly fanned out, some bearing to the right, some to the left, staying concealed in the trees until the pond was hemmed in on three sides. Then Snake drew his revolver, waved it in a small circle overhead, and all the outlaws burst from cover with much whooping and hollering.

Aggie turned to stone. Sophia covered her breasts with her arms and screamed. Both Hugh and Connie shot upright, Hugh drawing his hog-leg as he spun toward Snake Haddock. But Haddock fired first. Hugh twisted when hit and instinctively let go of his gun to clasp his left shoulder.

Then the outlaws were there. Haddock, his features as hard as iron, deliberately rode into Hugh Jennings, bowling the grizzled man over. A few hard cases covered Connie, who stood in numb shock. Most of the riders had halted between the pond and the fire and were smirking lewdly at Aggie and Sophia. Aggie held her head high, her chin jutting defiantly, her breasts even more so, not embarrassed in the least at being caught buck naked.

"Damn you, Snake Haddock!" she shouted. "Is this any way to greet old friends?"

Snake dropped to the ground, stepped up to the wooden box, and gave it a solid kick. "Do old friends steal from each other, Aggie?"

Fargo was watching Hugh Jennings writhe and groan. A hard object jabbed into his ribs, and he looked down to discover Porter had a cocked gun against his side.

"Get down, mister. And no funny stuff."

On the other side another outlaw had his revolver trained.

His frustration climbing, Fargo slid off. Jessup dismounted and also covered him. He turned and smiled at Connie, who was as white as a sheet. "Fancy seeing you again."

Aggie, heedless of the lustful stares of the outlaws, surged out of the pond, her full figure dripping wet, and angrily pointed at Fargo. "You! You're still alive! Did you lead them here, you bastard?"

"Don't blame him, Aggie," Haddock said, wearing a patronizing smile. He pointed at the tracker. "Blame our new man, Burnett. He can track an ant over miles of solid rock."

Stopping next to the pile of clothes she had left lying on the grass, Aggie placed both hands on her hips and glared at Snake. "So what now, Mr. High-and-Mighty? Do you let these coyotes rape us and then skin us alive like you did those pilgrims with the wagon train?"

"I know you, woman. You'd like us to jump you," Haddock shot back. "You think it would give you a chance to grab one of our guns when our britches are down around our ankles." He chuckled. "You never miss a trick, Aggie. It's what I like about you the best."

"Do you like me enough to let us go?"

"I wouldn't go that far."

Fargo saw his Ovaro, the dun, and the rest of the Jennings's horses tied to trees northwest of the pond. The stallion was only twenty-five yards off, but it might as well be on the moon. At any moment one of the Jennings might mention his part in saving them and his goose would be cooked.

"Get yourself dressed," Snake directed Aggie. "I don't want you giving my men ideas when they should be paying attention to what they're doing." He gazed past her at Sophia. "You, too, gorgeous. And don't fret. No one will lay a hand on you while I'm alive."

"You always were partial to her," Aggie muttered.

"Only because Sophia doesn't think she has the God-given right to nag a man to death once she goes to bed with him," Haddock said. "She knows how to behave herself, which is more than I can say for you. Now get those clothes on and don't cause trouble or I'll shoot a couple of you to make my point." Pivoting, he aimed his revolver at the Trailsman and cocked the hammer. "Starting with him."

8

Agatha Jennings nodded. "You want to kill this no-account polecat, you go right ahead."

Fargo's eyes were glued to Snake Haddock's trigger finger. If it started to tighten, he would throw himself to the side in a desperate bid to avoid taking lead.

"You wouldn't mind?" the outlaw leader asked, his brow knit as he regarded Aggie skeptically.

"Mind, hell! I wanted him dead. I thought he was a goner after I walloped him with my rifle and he fell and cracked his skull on a boulder," Aggie said, frowning. "I knew I should have gone down and checked but Pa was certain he was dead."

"Why did you try to kill him?"

"Because he got too interested in the box for his own good," Aggie answered. "We had asked him to guide us out of the mountains. Then he took to studying on the box, looking at it when he thought we wouldn't notice. But we knew he would try to take a peek inside. So when he made the mistake of telling us we were almost to the foothills, we decided we didn't need his help anymore." She bent down to pick up her clothes, and one of the outlaws whistled in appreciation.

Hugh Jennings, his eyes closed, his face flushed, moaned and rolled onto his side.

"Quit your bellyaching," Snake snapped, slowly lowering his revolver. He let the hammer down and winked at Fargo. "You'll live for a while yet, mister." Then, without warning, he hauled off and kicked Hugh in the back.

Jennings stiffened and cried out. He struggled to sit up, his hand covering his wound, his fingers coated with blood. "Can't you see how bad off I am?" he whined. "Only you would kick a man when he's down!"

"I'll do it again if you get me mad," Snake warned and angrily indicated the wooden box. "I should gut you right here and now for what you did. But I want you to suffer first. I want to pay you back for all you've put us through." He slid his pistol in his holster. "Before I'm done, you'll beg me to put you out of your misery."

Connie, who until that moment had not so much as twitched a muscle, now took a step and shook the ladle she held at Haddock. "Why don't you just take the stinking box and leave us alone? You've shot Pa. Isn't that enough?"

"Not on your life, missy," Haddock said. He studied her, chewing on his lower lip until finally he sighed. "This wasn't your idea, was it?"

"Need you ask?"

"I figured as much. I'm inclined to let you live, Connie, if you give me your word you'll leave this part of the country and never, ever, come back."

"We're a family, Snake. We stick together no matter what. You know that."

"I reckon I do," Snake Haddock said and stepped around the fire to pour himself a cup of coffee.

Fargo spied his Sharps propped on a saddle behind Haddock. His Colt was tucked under Snake's black leather belt. If only he could get his hands on them! Most of the outlaws were watching Agatha and Sophia dress. Sophia had turned her back to them, but Aggie brazenly donned her clothes for all to see. He looked at Connie, who caught his eye and nodded almost imperceptibly at the outlaw leader. What was she trying to get across? he wondered.

"You would have had a fair share," Snake addressed Hugh. "But that wasn't enough for you. You had to go whole hog." He took a loud sip and smacked his lips. "Good coffee, Connie, as usual."

There was genuine warmth in Haddock's expression when he spoke, and Fargo realized that here was a man who had a soft spot for women. Some outlaws, the very worst of the rabid killers, would as soon shoot a woman as a man; it made no difference to them. Haddock was a different breed, the sort who could put lead into a man without blinking an eye but who had a hard time killing women even when he believed it was necessary.

"I'm making stew," Connie said, moving to the pot. "I doubt we have enough for everyone, but you're more than welcome to have some."

"Don't mind if I do," Snake said politely.

Smiling demurely, Connie began stirring the stew. The broth was bubbling. She glanced up at Fargo and again inclined her head ever so slightly toward Snake.

Fargo thought he understood. She was about to do something that would give him a fleeting chance to grab his Colt or another weapon. Jessup, Porter, and the gunman who had been covering him were all watching Agatha and Sophia. He edged to the left, closer to the fire, and casually sidled nearer to Snake Haddock. None of the outlaws objected. Aggie was only half-dressed, her ample breasts swaying as she moved.

"I haven't had a bite all day," Snake said and swallowed more coffee. He twisted to regard Aggie, his eyes lit by inner mirth. "That gal missed her mark. She should work the streets in St. Louis or New Orleans. Hell, in a year she'd be as rich as she ever dreamed of being."

"Possibly," Connie said, ladling stew into a bowl. She filled it to the brim, then dropped the ladle into the pot.

With the hungry eyes of every outlaw present devouring Aggie and Sophia as they dressed, no one except Fargo had noticed that Connie filled the bowl with almost all broth. The steaming liquid was scorching hot. So he almost felt sorry for Snake Haddock when Connie suddenly whirled and tossed the stew into Snake's face, directly into the outlaw leader's eyes. He sprang the moment Connie began her turn, reaching Snake in a single bound and yanking the Colt free. A quick step took him behind Snake, the Colt touching Haddock's temple, and he crouched down.

Snake's automatic response had been to roar like a wounded bear and to press both hands to his eyes. When the barrel of the Colt touched his skin, he went rigid, his eyes still covered, broth running down his cheeks and dripping from his beard.

The outlaws whirled, many extending their revolvers.

"Don't!" Fargo bellowed. "Even if you hit me, Haddock will die!"

For several seconds the outcome hung in the balance. Most of the outlaws risked hitting Haddock if they fired. Only three of them had a clear shot at Fargo, and they knew if they did he might squeeze the trigger in sheer reflex. So all nine of them hesitated, and in the tense seconds that ensued Snake Haddock's voice rang out forceful and clear.

"No one shoot! The man who does answers to me!"

"Lower your guns!" Fargo added and jammed the Colt harder into Haddock's temple to stress his point. Porter was the first to do so. Reluctantly, Burnett and the others complied.

Bo Jessup was the last to lower his six-shooter, his face blazing hatred. "You're crazy, mister, if you think you can get away from us. Make it easy on yourself and drop your gun."

Fargo ignored him. "Now toss your guns in the pond," he ordered.

"Like hell we will," Porter said.

Jessup nodded. "The only way anyone will ever get my gun will be to pry it from my stiff fingers."

"I'll shoot Haddock," Fargo warned.

Porter shook his head. "No, I don't reckon you will. If you shoot him, there's nothing to stop us from filling you with enough lead to drop a buffalo in its tracks."

Snake Haddock gave a short laugh. "Looks like you outfoxed yourself, Fargo. Now what are you going to do?"

That was the question uppermost on Fargo's mind. Porter was right. He didn't dare shoot Haddock or the rest would open fire. And if he couldn't make them drop their guns, sooner or later one of the outlaws would become impatient and try to nail him. Bo Jessup was just itching to try, he could tell. His only other option was to start blasting the outlaws, but he'd only be able to get three or four of them before the rest downed him on the spot. It was a no-win situation.

He noticed Connie had been edging to his right. None of the outlaws were concerned about her; they were all watching him. She moved to his rear, seemingly to remove herself from the line of fire, her hands at her waist, her head bowed, the empty bowl in her right hand. He was aware she had stopped, then he saw Porter's eyes widen in alarm a heartbeat before he heard the distinct click of a hammer being pulled back.

"What are you fixing to do with that cannon?" Porter asked.

Connie stepped into view again, the Sharps leveled at Porter's chest. "I want every last man to ride out right this minute. If you don't, I swear to heaven I'll drop you before I go down."

Porter licked his lips and glanced at Snake.

"You heard the lady," Fargo prompted, grateful for her help. He put himself in Porter's boots and knew what the man must be thinking. At that range, the Sharps would blow a hole in Porter big enough to stick a fist through. Some of the outlaws were fidgeting nervously, upset by the turn of events.

Haddock chuckled. "I never figured you had this much grit, Connie. But I should have known. You always were the quiet one, and it's the quiet ones who are always full of little surprises."

"What do you want us to do, Snake?" Porter asked.

Suddenly Aggie darted forward and scooped up the revolver her father had dropped when Haddock shot him. A wicked grin animating her features, she cocked the gun and trained it in the general direction of Burnett and two other outlaws. "Be damn sure you make the right choice, Snake, or you won't have a gang left to speak of."

Haddock started to move his head, then stopped and asked, "Mind if I lower my hands a mite?"

"Do it slow," Fargo cautioned.

"Don't worry. I'm not anxious to get myself killed," Snake said, easing his hands to his chin. He glanced up at Connie, then at Aggie, and finally at Porter. "It appears they hold all the high cards for the moment. Ride off. You know what to do."

Porter nodded and took a step backward, toward his horse. "All right. You heard the man. Mount and ride west."

"No!" Bo Jessup snarled. "We can take them! It's just one man and a pair of skirts!"

"Do as Porter says," Haddock snapped. "If you start anything, I'll be the first one to fall." He nodded at their horses. "Get the hell out of here. You'll have your chance soon enough."

Fargo waited until they were all mounted before he straightened. He held the Colt against Haddock's temple as the outlaws rode into the trees. Agatha cackled in triumph. He wasn't quite so pleased. The outlaws still had their guns, and they weren't about to give up until they freed their leader. Bending down, he relieved Haddock of his pistol and took a step back. "The first sign of trouble—," he began.

Suddenly there was a shout in the trees, and Bo Jessup burst from the undergrowth at a full gallop. He held a rifle that he pressed to his right shoulder as he charged.

Fargo shifted and raised both revolvers. He would rather have used the Sharps, but the distance was only twenty-five yards, and a revolver, in the hands of an expert, could drop a man at seventy-five. He fired the Colt and Haddock's pistol at the same moment the rifle boomed. Jessup's shot missed. Fargo's two slugs took effect, tearing into Jessup's chest and flipping the rash outlaw over the back of his horse. Jessup crashed down hard and lay sprawled with his left leg bent at an unnatural angle.

"Damn fool!" Snake muttered.

Fargo faced the forest. Porter appeared, his hands held palms out to show he meant no harm.

"That was Bo's doing and his alone!" he yelled. "I tried to stop him but he wouldn't listen." He gripped his reins. "I just wanted you to know so you wouldn't plug Snake." With that, he vanished in the pines.

"Now there's a good man," Snake said.

Aggie walked over and pointed her gun at him. "I don't care what Porter says. You were fixing to kill us, so it's only right that I repay the favor and put a bullet in your brain."

Fargo turned. "No. You can't kill him now."

"Why the hell not?"

"Think. Once he's dead, what's to stop his men from attacking us?"

"We can take them."

Hugh Jennings had risen to his knees. He glared at his daughter and rasped out, "Curse your contrary nature, girl! Use your head, like the Trailsman says. We need

Snake alive until we can figure a way to lose the rest of those bastards." His face became red and he doubled over, groaning. Sophia and Connie were immediately at his side.

Haddock glanced up at Fargo in surprise. "Did I hear right? Are you the one they call the Trailsman?"

Fargo nodded.

"Damn. This day is chock full of surprises. I should have made the connection sooner. But you never told us your first name. *Skye* Fargo, isn't it?"

Again Fargo nodded. "If I had told you, what would you have done?"

Snake grinned. "I would have left you where I found you, only we would have used you for target practice first."

Fargo slid his Colt into his holster and stepped around Haddock to take the Sharps from Connie. She was kneeling beside Hugh, who was stretched out, his shirt soaked with blood. "How bad is it?" he asked.

Hugh swallowed. "I can ride, if that's what you're wondering."

"We have to stop the bleeding first," Sophia said. "You'll bleed to death if we don't."

"Unbutton his shirt," Fargo directed. "Let's have a look." He stared at Aggie. "Keep Snake covered while we patch up your pa."

"My pleasure."

Hugh Jennings was in bad shape. The bullet had missed vital organs but torn an artery. The blood kept pouring out. There was no exit wound, so the slug was still inside him.

Fargo gave Haddock's revolver and the Sharps to Sophia. He was about to draw his Arkansas toothpick when he remembered that Snake wore a hunting knife in a leather sheath on his left hip. Going over, he plucked the knife out. Haddock made no move to stop him. "Almost forgot this," he said, and leaned over to heat the blade in the fire. The women anxiously observed his every move. When he judged the blade hot enough, he sank to one knee next to Hugh and probed the bullet hole with his fingers. The slug was two inches under the skin and wedged fast. "This will hurt," he stated.

"No foolin'," Hugh responded. "Just do what you've

got to. I'll survive. I always do." He picked up his shirt and clamped down on part of a sleeve with his teeth.

Fargo wasted no time. He carefully inserted the blade and pried the hole open wide enough to extract the slug. Hugh threw back his head when the scorching steel first touched his skin with a loud hiss, then clenched his fists until the knuckles were white and tried to hold himself still. The slug proved difficult to get out, and Fargo's hands were coated in blood before he was through. He tossed the slug aside, then heated the knife once more.

Hugh had relaxed his mouth and was panting heavily. "Sweet Jesus!" he wheezed. "I'm gettin' too old for nonsense like this."

The blade glowed when Fargo took his position and poised it over the wound. "I have to stop the blood now," he said.

"Where's a pint of whiskey when a man needs it?" Hugh joked, and bit down on the shirt.

The smell of burning flesh filled the air. By pressing the red-hot blade against both sides of the hole, Fargo successfully cauterized the wound. The bleeding had stopped when he stood and wiped a hand across his perspiring forehead. "There. All done."

"Thanks. I'm in your debt," Hugh said weakly.

Sophia gazed quizzically at Fargo. "I don't understand you. We tried to kill you back on that mountain, yet you helped Pa by digging out that lead. Why?"

"It had to be done," Fargo said, and let his answer go at that. They would only become mad if they knew his true motive, namely that he wanted to get out of there before the outlaws tried to pick them off with rifles or used some other tactic to rescue Snake. And since the women weren't about to go anywhere with Hugh bleeding like a stuck pig, there had been no choice but to get Hugh in shape to ride. He gave the knife to Connie, then spied a lariat among the stacked supplies and carried it over to Haddock. "Hold your hands out behind you," he commanded.

Sighing, Snake did as he was told. He grunted when the rope was looped around his wrists. "Not so tight. You'll cut off my circulation," he groused.

"That's the general idea," Fargo replied. He tied the

knots good and tight. "Aggie, you and Sophia bring the horses over. We'll load up and head due east."

"Who put you in charge?" Aggie asked.

Connie took a step toward her. "He's the only one who can get us out of this mess alive. Stop giving him such a hard time and do as he says."

"You're sticking up for him?" Aggie smirked. "And you backed his play when he was cornered. Why, little sister, if I didn't know better, I'd swear you were in love. Don't tell me you finally let a man get under your dress?" Tossing back her head, she laughed.

No one was more shocked at what transpired next than Agatha. Connie took two swift strides and swung her right hand with all her might. The slap rang out like a gunshot, and Aggie staggered, a hand over her cheek.

"Don't you ever talk to me like that again!" Connie raged, shaking a fist. "I'm sick and tired of listening to your filthy mouth and putting up with your harlot ways! If you want to be a slut, that's your business. But don't expect all of us to live like you do!"

"A slut?" Aggie blurted, and would have closed on Connie if not for Sophia, who moved between them and held her hands out to keep them from each other's throat.

Fargo couldn't believe they were squabbling at a time when all of their lives were in danger. He went to intervene when Hugh bellowed in fury.

"Enough, damn your hides! You can tear each other's hair out later! Right now we have to skedaddle, before Porter and the rest try something! Aggie and Sophia, get the damn horses! Connie, give me a hand puttin' my shirt on."

They were a grim lot as they hurriedly loaded the pack animals and saddled their horses. Fargo and Connie helped Hugh mount. Then Fargo put Haddock astride the outlaw's own horse and swung onto the Ovaro, the trailing end of the rope in his left hand along with the Sharps.

None of the outlaws showed themselves as Fargo headed eastward, skirting the pond and entering forest beyond. He was certain Porter would try to free Haddock before they reached the plains. The attack could come at any time, from any direction. In order to make it harder on the outlaws, he stuck to the high ground, going over hills instead of around them, using the high ground to his advantage by stopping often to scour the countryside.

An hour passed uneventfully. Fargo's stomach dearly desired food, but he couldn't let down his guard for a minute. They came to a stream, crossed over, and rode to the crest of a bald hill where he reined up.

"We're stopping again?" Aggie complained.

"I'm not one to ride into an ambush," Fargo told her, studying the land ahead. His gut instinct warned him to be extra wary. He saw nothing to confirm the feeling, but he had learned never to discount his sixth sense. Many frontiersmen and most Indians had it, born of living life in the raw among wild beasts and treacherous enemies. A man never knew if death might be lurking over the next rise or around the next bend in the trail, so he learned to ride with care.

He started down, the Ovaro six feet ahead of Haddock's mount. His head had taken to hurting again a short while ago and now throbbed. He wanted to adjust his hat to see if the pain would be reduced, but he needed his hands free in case his hunch proved to be right. The woods below were somber and still, too still. No birds were singing. There were no squirrels playing in the trees.

Fargo glanced back. Snake Haddock was yawning. Sophia was next to Hugh, who swayed precariously every few feet and might keel over at any moment. Connie led the pack animals. Agatha, a rifle clasped in her right hand, brought up the rear.

He angled to the south, where the forest was thickest. Off to the north a pair of robins flew toward the hill. They altered course, making for the trees, and were about to alight when, uttering frightened chirps, they arced upward and sped off.

Fargo halted. Something had frightened those birds. It could have been a bobcat or some other animal. Or it could have been Haddock's gang waiting in concealment for him to ride into their gun sights.

"What's the matter, Trailsman?" Haddock taunted him. "Are you yellow?"

"Get in front of me," Fargo said, pulling on the lariat. Using his legs to guide his horse, Haddock did as he was instructed. He grinned at Fargo as he went past. "You're not long for this world. I hope you know that."

"If I go down, so do you," Fargo vowed. He resumed the descent, his nerves tingling. They were thirty yards from the tree line when Aggie yelled.

"Behind us!"

One look showed him four outlaws racing over the top of the hill. He dug his spurs into the pinto and faced front just as rifles thundered in the pines.

9

"Get to cover!" Fargo shouted and galloped like mad toward the forest, straight into the firing guns. Out in the open he didn't stand a prayer. And if he veered to either side he would present a better target to the hidden riflemen. At least among the trees he would have some cover and be better able to defend himself. He hunched low over the saddle and swept past Snake Haddock, who was trying to keep his animal from bolting.

Behind him rose the shrill whinny of a horse, then a terrified scream.

Agatha's rifle boomed.

Fargo was twisting to glance over his shoulder when his worst nightmare was realized. The Ovaro was hit! He felt the stallion's blood splatter on his face and saw its head jerk back, and then his left arm was wrenched backward as the lariat was torn from his grasp. He looked and saw that Snake Haddock had intentionally thrown himself to the ground. He also saw Hugh's horse and Connie's were both down. Aggie was surrounded by the four outlaws who had come over the crest. And Sophia sat astride her standing mount, paralyzed with fear, her hands upraised.

A second later the stallion was among the pines, running flat out in a rare panic heightened by its agony. Fargo glimpsed a figure to his right, another to his left. Rifles cracked. A bullet smacked into a limb within inches of his head. Others buzzed like angry hornets. He rose high enough to level the Sharps at a third outlaw almost directly in his path. The big rifle belched lead and smoke. The outlaw, struck in the stomach, clutched at his abdomen and toppled.

A thicket loomed ahead, but the Ovaro made no effort

to avoid it. In moments they had crashed through, the thin branches tearing at the stallion's legs and belly. To their rear a woman shrieked. A few rifle shots shattered the air, then the sounds of conflict ended.

Fargo straightened and hauled on the reins, but for the first time ever the pinto refused to respond and kept on at breakneck speed. Another drop of blood spattered on his cheek. He let the stallion go unchecked for another mile, giving it time to get the fear out of its system, until they emerged from the forest into a spacious meadow. Then he hauled on the reins again. At last the Ovaro came to a stop, its sides heaving, its head drooping as it snorted and stamped a front hoof.

Swinging down, Fargo jammed the Sharps in its scabbard to free his hands. He saw a crimson streak on the stallion's neck. Closer examination revealed how lucky they had been. The bullet had dug a half-inch-deep furrow over six inches in length but had not penetrated the pinto's flesh or hit a major artery. He stroked it and spoke softly until it calmed.

A stand of spruce beside a bubbling brook seventy yards away drew his attention. Climbing up, he rode over. His mind was in turmoil as he cut a strip off his blanket and used it to dab water on the stallion's wound.

The Jennings family must be either dead or prisoners. He had tried his best, but it hadn't been enough. Since he'd known he couldn't hope to lose the outlaws, not when Burnett was such a skilled tracker, he had hoped to get out on the plains where he could see an attack coming from a long ways off and where they were more likely to run into other whites and friendly Indians. So much for his plan.

He had to admit that he honestly felt little sympathy for any of the Jennings with the notable exception of Connie. Hugh and Aggie had plotted to kill him. Sophia had been interested in him as a means to satisfy her insatiable sexual cravings, and for no other reason. Of them all, only Connie had offered him true friendship, and it bothered him to think of her in Snake Haddock's hands.

Then there was Haddock himself. It galled Fargo to think that the outlaw had won out, had beaten him, had gotten the Jennings and the gold and could now do as he damn well pleased. Fargo didn't like losing. He was a born fighter, a man who never took anything lying down, who never allowed anyone to ride roughshod over him, and who couldn't turn his back on a friend in need.

He knew what he was going to do. He could no more mount up and ride off without doing something than he could just stop breathing. He was going to save Connie or die trying.

Fargo let the stallion drink and opened his saddlebags to take out a bundle of jerky he'd obtained at Fort Benton. He was ravenous and ate the strips greedily, wishing he had a venison steak instead.

Suddenly, in the forest, a squirrel chattered angrily.

The jerky was forgotten as Fargo grabbed the pinto's reins and took the stallion in among the spruce trees. Not a moment too soon. He peered at the forest and spied three riders moving through the shadows. They halted shy of the meadow to scan the waving grass. Then they slowly emerged, all three carrying rifles. In the lead was none other than Burnett.

A thin smile curled Fargo's lips as he stuffed the jerky into his saddlebags, drew his Sharps out, and removed the spare Sharps from his bedroll. He swiftly loaded both rifles, leaned the one that had belonged to Harvey Stone against a trunk, and pressed his own rifle to his right shoulder. A tingle of satisfaction coursed through him as he took a bead on Burnett's chest.

The three outlaws came on cautiously. Burnett was reading the sign, bent forward to better see the soil. He glanced at the brook, then at the stand of spruce trees, but saw nothing to arouse concern.

Fargo let them come. He cocked the hammer, set the trigger, and waited until they were ten yards from the brook. "Looking for someone?" he shouted and fired.

Burnett had snapped upright at the shout. His eyes widened and he was attempting to bring his rifle to bear when the slug bored through his torso, coring his heart.

The other two men also brought their rifles into play, but they shot hastily at the smoke in the stand and missed.

In a smooth motion, Fargo grabbed the second Sharps and placed his own against the tree. He had another outlaw in his sights before either could fire again. His slug blew the top of the man's head off.

Apparently deciding he wanted to live, the third outlaw wheeled his horse and made for the forest.

Fargo was in no mood to be merciful. His fingers flew as he worked the trigger guard and reloaded the Sharps. The outlaw was forty yards off and rapidly increasing the distance, but he wasn't worried. Forty yards or four hundred made no difference. He raised the rifle, sighted, and fired.

In the act of looking back, the outlaw threw up his arms and fell.

Five down, five to go, Fargo thought, collecting both rifles and reloading them, then placing them on the pinto. The odds were no longer so formidable. Mounting, he rode to the west, swinging in a wide loop that would eventually bring him back to the hill where the outlaws had sprung their ambush. He was filled with a fiery resolve to give Snake Haddock a taste of his own medicine.

Conscious of how the stallion must be hurting, he held the pinto to a walk, stopping every so often to wipe off its neck. A trickle of blood kept seeping out of the furrow, and he had no way to stop it. A bandage would be impractical.

The azure afternoon sky was bright with sun, but the breeze had picked up and lining the western horizon were ominous gray and black clouds. A storm was brewing. Before night rain would fall.

He reached the hill within an hour, approaching from the southwest with the Colt in his right hand. At the edge of the trees on the far side he halted to listen and to note the wildlife in the area. On the hill chipmunks frolicked. A raven flew over the crest and made no change in its flight, as it would if there was a large group of humans below.

Satisfied the outlaws were gone, Fargo rode higher, slid down to the ground below the crest, and walked forward until he could see the opposite slope. The first thing he saw were the dead horses, both Hugh's and Connie's, lying amidst pools of blood. He surveyed the slope carefully and was about convinced the outlaws had taken all of the Jennings clan with them when he saw the leg. It jutted out from behind a small boulder near where Hugh's horse lay.

He climbed back on the pinto and went to investigate. Hugh Jennings was flat on his back, his eyes open and tongue distended. His fingers had been cut off, then he had been stabbed multiple times in parts of his body that would not have caused immediate death. Someone had wanted him to suffer, and suffer greatly. As if all that wasn't enough, Hugh had also been gutted like a fish. His innards had spilled out over his midsection, oozing gastric juices over his pants and shirt.

A shadow flitted over the earth.

Skye glanced up and spied the first of the buzzards that would soon gather. It was circling, waiting for him to leave. He obliged, going to the base of the hill where he found the trail left by the departing outlaws. They had left within the past thirty minutes, he deduced, heading northeast.

Why northeast? Fargo mused as he started in pursuit. Fort Benton lay many miles in that direction. Otherwise, there was a vast expanse of prairie inhabited by various tribes and teeming with buffalo and antelope. Nothing that should particularly interest the likes of Snake Haddock.

He found a set of hoof prints that was deeper than it should be and concluded that Connie was riding double with one of the outlaws. For the next ninety minutes he trailed them, at which point the tracks bore on a more easterly course, toward the plains. He didn't like that. If Haddock went out on the open prairie, it would be hard for him to get close to them.

That was a problem he must deal with later. For the moment he was more disturbed by the oncoming storm. A heavy rain would wipe out all trace of hoof prints, and the roiling black clouds advancing inexorably across the heavens promised a deluge.

Fargo rode faster. The Ovaro was barely bleeding and moved at its usual steady gait. He wanted to get close enough to keep the outlaws in sight until after the storm passed. A growing premature twilight goaded him on, and he guessed he was no more than five minutes behind Haddock's bunch when the first large raindrops pattered around him.

He pressed ahead. The rain increased, making the back of his neck wet and clammy. He hiked his buckskin shirt and pulled down his hat, heedless of a pang in his head. Strong winds shook the nearby trees, rustling the leaves. Bushes swayed. The grass danced wildly.

In the distance thunder roared.

Fargo still hadn't overtaken the outlaws when the storm erupted in all its elemental fury. The driving rain fell in pounding sheets, bending tree limbs and the undergrowth alike, drenching the earth and everything on it, including Fargo and the Ovaro.

Lightning lanced the heavens nonstop, alleviating the gloom with brilliant zigzag streaks. Thunder rolled almost continuously.

As much as the Trailsman didn't care to stop, he had to. A man on horseback tempted fate by being abroad when lightning raged. Many a rider had lost his life by stubbornly refusing to seek shelter during a storm, and he was of no mind to be one of them. Unfortunately, he was hemmed in by woodland. The only available shelter was under a tree, which could be just as dangerous as staying on horseback.

He squinted against the lashing raindrops and made out the outline of a huge tree on his left. Angling under it, he climbed down and held fast to the reins in case the lightning or thunder should spook the Ovaro. He squatted, braced his back against the wide trunk, and waited for the storm to end.

A jagged yellow bolt struck a high tree not thirty yards off. The Ovaro, ears pricked, nostrils flared, tried to pull loose and run but Fargo grasped the reins with both hands. Matters weren't helped by the tremendous crash of thunder that attended the lightning bolt. The Ovaro pulled harder, forcing Fargo to dig in his heels.

The storm seemed to rage forever. Despite the protective limbs above him, Fargo was soaked to the skin when the rain finally slackened and the wind abated. He rose stiffly, petted the stallion, and forked leather.

To the east the sky crackled and poured down torrents as the storm moved out over the plains.

Fargo moved to where the tracks should be, but there were none. He began a systematic search of the immediate vicinity, executing ever wider circles, but found nothing. As he had predicted, the rain had washed away every last trace.

Squaring his shoulders, he rode eastward. Haddock must have stopped too, so the outlaws shouldn't be too far in front of him. Even if they had forged on, he might catch up with them before dark.

The cool breeze caused him to shiver. He couldn't wait to stop somewhere and build a fire so he would be warm again.

Clouds continued to shroud the landscape. The sun never reappeared. Gradually the twilight became an inky darkness. He came to a clearing and halted. If he was right, he still had ten miles or more to cover before reaching the prairie. And since he didn't want to make camp out there, where the flames of a fire could be seen for miles, he decided to stop right where he was. Dawn would bring a new day, and if he rose early he could still locate the outlaws without too much trouble. He hoped.

His shuddering intensified as he collected what dry wood he could find, mostly small limbs he found under brush or screened by patches of weeds. His fingers trembled as he arranged the limbs and got a blaze going. Then he huddled over the crackling flames, getting as close as he dared, grinning as his buckskins gave off steam. He grew warm, but not warm enough. His body was terribly, terribly cold.

His wound and his hunger, his loss of blood and his exertions, the entire ordeal he had been through since Agatha knocked him off the shelf, had all taken their toll. He was weak and famished. The jerky barely whetted his appetite. He ate every last morsel of grub contained in his saddlebags, then made a pot of coffee.

At last, when he had downed a cup of scalding brew, he felt warmth return to his limbs. He downed two more cupfuls before he began to feel like his old self. But every so often he would experience a fleeting cold sensation that made him shiver. He hoped he wasn't becoming ill.

After drying his blankets, he spread them out next to the fire and sat down to turn in. He idly brushed his hat back with his left hand and was shocked at how hot his brow felt. He had a fever! To make sure the fire lasted as long as possible, he gathered additional wood and fed as much as he dared to the flames. Then he settled into his blankets, closed his eyes, and was instantly asleep.

The cry of a jay awakened him. He lay still, annoyed to find he was still intensely cold, and let the warmth of the sun on his face slowly revive him. Suddenly he realized what that meant. Sitting up, he was stunned at seeing the sun a good two hours above the eastern horizon. He had slept the whole night through and well into the morning. Mad at himself, he went to stand when a wave of dizziness assailed him. He sat still, waiting for it to pass.

Why did he feel so weak? He raised his hand to his face and was startled to find his skin was even hotter than it had been last night. Then why did he still feel cold deep inside? Propping both hands on the ground, he rose to his knees, then carefully straightened. The Ovaro was right where he had left it, cropping grass.

He turned to the fire, which was now smoldering embers, and piled on branches left over from those he gathered before turning in. After considerable effort he was rewarded with crackling flames. His next chore was to make a fresh pot of coffee. Moving helped to warm him and gave him the impression his strength was returning.

Once the fragrant aroma filled the air, he searched his saddlebags but found nothing to eat. He was accustomed to living off the land, but in his current condition he decided it would be better to hold off doing any hunting until later in the day. A first cup of coffee did wonders to further invigorate him.

Four cups later he decided to saddle the stallion and make up for lost time. Lifting the saddle, though, required all the energy he could muster. Even folding and rolling his blankets took a lot out of him. When he finally climbed on the pinto, he was barely strong enough to stay upright.

Turning eastward, he kneed the Ovaro and rode in search of Haddock's trail. The downpour had barely quenched the soil's thirst, and the ground was once again hard. Except for a few downed limbs and a tree rent by lightning, there was scant evidence the storm had passed by.

Traveling five miles took so much out of him that he

stopped again to rest. As this rate, he wryly reflected, it wouldn't take more than a month to catch the outlaws. He must try harder. There was no telling what fate Snake had in store for the three women, but it was bound to be unpleasant. And since Connie had backed his play back at the pond, Snake might come up with something particularly nasty for her.

He rested five minutes. Mounting, he forged on. His body was no longer cold. Now he burned with fever and broke out in a sweat over every square inch of skin. Worse, his vision became blurred. He rubbed the back of his sleeve across his eyes. He squinted. He closed his eyes for a minute. Nothing helped. After a bit his vision returned to normal of its own accord. But he was upset that it might happen again.

An eternity seemed to go by.

At long last the trees thinned and he spied open land ahead. The plains! he realized. Elated, he rode to the edge of the prairie and halted to take in the limitless expanse of tall grass. There was no sign of the outlaws. He bore to the left, scouring the ground, confident he would find tracks soon enough.

Fargo stopped to ponder the chance that Haddock had swung even farther south. He could backtrack and see. But as Fargo turned the stallion another bout of dizziness struck. He reined up, swaying in the saddle, and grasped the saddle horn to steady himself. Strangely, it did no good. His body went completely limp, and then he saw the ground sweeping up to meet him.

What had happened? Skye wondered as his mind flicked back to life. He opened his eyes and saw the sky, a sky now gray when it should be bright blue. Puzzled, he rose on his elbows. The sun hovered above the western horizon. He had been unconscious most of the day!

Stunned, he pushed to his feet. The ever dependable pinto had not wandered far. It was forty feet off, grazing. Wind in his hair made him aware his hat had fallen off, so he bent over to retrieve it. More dizziness swamped him. Uttering a groan, he sank to his hands and knees.

What the hell was wrong? he fumed. Did he have pneumonia? He'd never had it, but he'd known men who had and all the symptoms were the same. Chills. High fever. A pain in his chest. He wasn't coughing yet, but that might come later.

Fargo sat down and took stock. If he did have pneumonia, he was in bad shape.

He tried not to think of what might be happening to Connie. The outlaws were a full day ahead of him and were bound to increase their lead before he recovered enough to give chase. Of all the times for him to take sick! Gritting his teeth, he stood and shuffled toward the stallion. The Ovaro gave him a quizzical look, as if it couldn't understand why he was walking so oddly. He took hold of the reins and leaned on the saddle to gird himself for the next step. "Hello, big fella," he said weakly, surprised at how strained his voice sounded.

The Ovaro bobbed its head.

Three attempts and he was able to mount. He leaned down, clinging to the saddle horn, and brought the pinto around. Camping on the prairie would be suicide. Hostiles might see the fire and they'd find him easy pickings. So he went into the trees and rode until a small clearing appeared. He'd hoped to find a stream but he lacked the resolve to keep on going.

Fargo sighed as he slid off. He was so hungry he could eat a bull elk at one sitting. When he tried to remove the Sharps, though, he was too weak. Exasperated, he staggered into the pines and sought limbs for a fire. A rabbit bounded out from the undergrowth and sped off. Instinctively, he clawed at his Colt, but his arm moved in slow motion. The rabbit was long gone before he could draw.

He made his way back to the clearing. His vision blurred once again, and it was all he could do to avoid the trees in his path. Vaguely, Fargo made out the shape of the stallion and tottered closer. Suddenly he saw another figure, a two-legged shape, come out of the trees on the other side of the clearing. With a start he perceived it was an Indian.

That was the last thing he remembered.

10

Fargo heard someone chanting softly. He was about to sit up when he recalled the figure he had seen and how sick he was. Better to play possum, he reasoned. If warriors from a hostile tribe had captured him, they might begin torturing him the second he revived. He listened intently, trying to determine how many there were and to which tribe they belonged.

"You can open your eyes, white man. I will not scalp you."

Bewildered, Fargo remained still. How did they know he was awake? The man who had just spoken had used flawless English, which was interesting. Only peaceful Indians ever got that good at the white man's tongue.

"If you want to pretend you are still asleep, then do so," the warrior said. "White men are always doing strange things. I just thought you might like some soup."

There was a humorous, friendly quality to the voice that prompted Skye to do as the man wanted. He beheld a white-haired Shoshoni whose face contained a wrinkle for each year of life he must have lived, squatting beside a fire not a yard away.

"Ah, so you do have some manners. With white men one never knows. Most of your kind are so in love with themselves that they have not yet learned how to be human beings."

Fargo didn't know whether to laugh or feel insulted.

"Can you speak? Or is your tongue as weak as your brain?" The old warrior picked up a crude bark bowl sitting near the fire. "Would you like some soup? You should eat something after all you have been through."

"Who are you?" Fargo croaked.

"He talks!" the warrior declared and grinned. "My

patience is rewarded." He moved closer, careful not to spill the contents of the bowl. "My name, white man, is Beaver Tail. And before you ask, I will tell you that I learned your miserable tongue from a missionary who visited my people many winters ago. He was strange, too, always trying to get us to believe in the white man's God when we were perfectly happy worshiping the Great Medicine Spirit as we have always done." He lowered his voice as if confiding a secret. "I never told him, but I suspect that your God and the Great Medicine Spirit are one and the same. I do not yet know why the Spirit saw fit to give my people more wisdom than yours, but that is the way things are."

"What—?" Fargo began, trying to get a word in edgewise.

"Save your questions until you have eaten," Beaver Tail chided. "You must still be weak after being sick for so long." He held the bowl under Fargo's nose. "Squirrel soup. It is delicious, if I do say so myself. I had to search hard to find the right herbs." He paused. "I even added some ants for flavoring."

The odor was tantalizing. Fargo's mouth watered as he inhaled deeply. Then the full force of his hunger hit him with the impact of a hammer, wrenching his gut and causing a brief nausea. He grimaced and touched his stomach.

"What is wrong?" Beaver Tail asked. "Are you one of those squeamish whites who will not eat anything but deer, elk, and buffalo meat? Squirrel meat is delicious, almost as good as mountain lion meat."

"It smells fine," Fargo said, putting his left elbow down so he could lift the upper half of his body. "I haven't eaten in a while, is all."

"Longer than you think, white man."

"What do you mean?"

"You have been sick for six days."

Fargo, without thinking, sat up. "Six days!" he exclaimed in amazement, the movement compounding the nausea. "Are you sure?"

"Why is it that white men always ask such stupid questions?" Beaver Tail rejoined. He sadly shook his head. "If I live a hundred winters, I will never understand why the Great Medicine Spirit saw fit to make more of your people than my people. It makes better sense to have more smart people than dumb ones."

"Six days?" Fargo repeated, dazed by the implications. By now Snake Haddock was long gone, and any hope he had entertained of saving Constance Jennings was shattered.

"You like those words, do you?" Beaver Tail said, and chuckled. "Six days. Six Days. They do have a fine sound to them. As fine as any words in your raven tongue. I must confess I had no idea men could chatter like birds until I first heard white men speak." He gestured with the bowl. "Now take this, please, and eat."

Mentally awhirl, Fargo gripped the bark bowl and tilted it to sip the hot soup, which was every bit as delicious as the Shoshoni had claimed.

"Why are you so upset? Many men do not survive the breathing sickness. You would have been helpless on your own. If I had not found you, you would now be dead."

"Thanks," Fargo mumbled, savoring the taste of the first real meal he had enjoyed in over a week. He gazed into the warrior's lively brown eyes and smiled. "I'm in your debt, old-timer. My name is Skye Fargo."

"For a white man's name, yours is as musical as those of my people," Beaver Tail said, and motioned for Skye to keep eating.

Fargo ate in silence, taking his sweet time, knowing to rush would only make him sick. He was glad to be alive, glad the pneumonia had subsided, but bitter over his failure to rescue Connie. Ever since he'd met the Jennings family, he had suffered one setback after another. This was the last straw.

Beaver Tail was studying him. "You are a deep thinker. I can tell. That is good, because too few whites bother to exercise their brains. They would rather lie in a lodge all day with a woman than try to understand life. Perhaps that is why your kind is so intent on rubbing out everything that lives."

"You don't sound very fond of white men," Fargo commented.

"Had it been up to me, I would have made all of you go away before you could breed like rabbits and take the land. But my people have always taken pride in being your friends." He frowned. "I thought for a while about joining another tribe, but my wife said no others would have me."

Now Fargo did laugh, long and hard.

"Be careful," Beaver Tail warned. "Do not exert yourself. Your fever is gone, but you will need time to regain your strength. Take two or three days to rest. I will stay and feed you until you are fit enough to ride."

"I'm riding out tomorrow morning," Fargo said, gazing up at the sun which was directly overhead. The rest of the day and one night was all the time he could spare. Delayed or not, he was going to go after Snake Haddock anyway. And if anything had happened to Connie, he would make certain Haddock's reign of terror ended. Hell, he would make certain in any event.

"Are you as crazy as most whites? You need more rest," the Shoshoni said. "Have I gone to all this trouble for nothing? I gave you medicine and nursed you as if you were my own son. Why must you leave so soon?"

Between sips Fargo related his run-in with the Jennings family and the outlaws. He finished, then drank the last bit of soup and licked his lips. "I have to find those women. No matter how long it takes, no matter how many miles I have to cover, I'll hunt down Snake Haddock and find out what happened to them."

"The one you call Haddock plans to sell them to renegades."

About to lower the bowl, Fargo glanced sharply at his newfound friend. "How do you know?"

"I heard them talking."

Fargo was all attention. "When and where?"

"The morning of the very day I came on your tracks and saw where you had fallen off your horse. From the shod hoofs and boot prints I knew you were a white man in trouble," Beaver Tail said. "I decided to follow you anyway and see what I could do." He chuckled. "It must have been the sun getting to me."

"Get to the point about the outlaws."

"Very well. I was on my way back to my village after failing to kill a buffalo when I saw them," Beaver Tail said, and digressed again. "My wife did not want me to go after a buffalo, but I had not hunted one in many winters and I missed the old thrill." He shook his head in disbelief. "I tried my best, but every buffalo I tried to shoot ran off before I could kill it. I could not believe how much faster buffalo are today than they were ten winters ago. Do you think they are eating a different kind of grass?"

"The outlaws, Beaver Tail. Tell me about the outlaws."

"Be patient, Skye Fargo. I am getting to them." The warrior pondered for a few seconds. "Let me see. I spotted them far to the north, riding along the tree line as was I, so I rode into the forest and sat there until they passed. I made no effort to hide but they rode by without seeing me." He paused. "I must have been invisible again."

"Invisible?"

"My spirit guardian gave me this power when I was a very young man. I had gone on a vision quest," Beaver Tail detailed matter-of-factly. "This is a wonderful power. I have used it many times in battle. All I need do is think the right words and I am completely invisible. If I am on my horse, it too is invisible." He scratched his chin. "Now that I am getting old, I sometimes think the words without paying attention to what I am doing and I turn invisible without knowing I have done so. It can be most embarrassing."

Fargo knew all about the Indian belief in a host of spirits that could be called on for assistance and how diligently warriors sought supernatural visions and the aid of supernatural beings, so he didn't laugh at the notion of the old brave turning invisible. "What did you hear when the outlaws went past?" he prompted, trying to get the warrior back on the matter that interested him the most.

"They were all chattering like chipmunks, as whites often do. I saw three women. Two were on horses by themselves, and the third rode with a big man who had a nose the size of a buffalo's. He wore a black hat and rode in the lead," Beaver Tail said. "None of the women seemed very happy. One was yelling at the big man, telling him she would cut off his balls if he tried to sell them to Minio—"

"Minio?" Fargo interrupted. He'd heard the name once or twice. It was the name of a renegade Cheyenne who had been thrown out of his tribe for murdering another Cheyenne, and who now rode with a small pack of other outcasts. The band numbered no more than four or five, but they had caused no end of grief by raiding isolated farms and ranches to butcher and rape. What was the connection between Snake Haddock and Minio?

"The big man told the woman to shut up. He told her that she had brought it on herself by turning against him. He also said he was sorry that her sisters must share her fate, but he could not afford to spare any of them. Those were his exact words."

"Did they say where they were meeting Minio?"

"No."

"Did they say when?"

"No. But one of the men did say he was worried about his horse going lame and they still had a long ride ahead of them."

"Then there's hope yet," Fargo said, more to himself than the Shoshoni. He glanced over at where the Ovaro stood beside a brown war pony well past its prime. His first impulse was to saddle up and ride in pursuit of the outlaws, but he risked suffering a relapse if he didn't get some more food into his belly and rest at least one more night.

"Do not worry. We will catch these evil men," Beaver Tail said.

Fargo looked at him. "We? This is my fight, not yours. I'm going after them alone."

"What if you become sick again? You will need me by your side to help."

"That's a chance I'll just have to take," Fargo said. "You're not coming and that's final."

The Shoshoni refused to back down. "Did you not say you are in my debt for saving your life?"

"Yes," Fargo admitted, "but—"

"Then you can repay your debt by taking me along," Beaver Tail stated. He grinned slyly. "Unless, like most whites, you are not a man of your word. I know how many of your kind speak lies with as little thought as my people give to breathing."

"There are other ways I can repay the debt," Fargo said. "I'll shoot buffalo for you, get you a better horse, or anything else I can do. But I'm not taking you along. Snake Haddock would torture you worse than the Apaches would if you should be caught."

"I am willing to face the danger."

"I'm not. So drop the subject," Fargo said testily.

"Please," Beaver Tail said. He placed his hand on Fargo's wrist. "You do not know how much this means to me. I have not gone on a raid or taken part in a battle for more than thirty winters. The young warriors all say I am too old, and none of them will let me ride with their war parties. They honor my wisdom, but behind my back they snicker at my fighting prowess." He gazed wistfully into the pines. "It was not always like this. When I was a young man, I was a mighty warrior. I counted thirty-four coup and stole many horses. I was respected by every Shoshoni." Sorrow lined his face. "This might be my last chance to relive those days. I can go back to my people and proudly tell them of my exploits. The young men will look up to me as they did when I was their age." He paused, choking on his words, his eyes misting over. "Please, Skye Fargo. I beg you."

Fargo sat back, his common sense telling him to be firm but his conscience pricking him into agreeing. "Don't beg," he said gruffly.

"Please."

The old man's fingers tightened on Fargo's wrist, and he scowled. Not at the Shoshoni, but at his own soft heart. "Damn!" he muttered, then nodded. "All right. You can tag along."

For one so old, Beaver Tail surged upright like a youth in his teens and proceeded to jump up and down, singing in his own tongue.

"Calm down," Fargo said. "You didn't let me finish. There are conditions you must follow."

Beaver Tail halted, his arms overhead. "What conditions would you set?"

"You'll do as I tell you every step of the way. If you give me guff, back you go. And you're not to take any risks. If there's fighting to be done, you leave it to me."

"May I fight if I am attacked?"

"If you have no other choice," Fargo said and couldn't understand why the warrior beamed like a kid who had just been given the birthday gift of his dreams. "Do you agree?"

"Yes, Skye Fargo. You have my promise that I will

do as you say. I will give you no reason to regret your decision."

"I hope not."

The rest of the day Fargo spent eating, drinking, and listening to Beaver Tail relate tales of his younger days. Fargo learned that the warrior and the missionary who had lived with the Shoshonis had been close friends, and that Beaver Tail had spent countless hours learning English from this man of the cloth. Back then the warrior had not been so critical of the white race. That all changed when the missionary, the fire and brimstone sort, got a young maiden pregnant. Filled with shame and remorse, the missionary refused to have anything more to do with the maiden and their half-breed child. The woman, on learning this, went off into the woods to grieve in private. She took the baby along. Both were killed by a grizzly. Shortly thereafter the missionary left, and Beaver Tail had never found it in his heart to forgive him.

The maiden had been Beaver Tail's niece.

Fargo turned in early to be fully refreshed for the next day. As he dozed off he saw the Shoshoni doing some sort of dance over by the pines. He mentally cursed himself for being fool enough to tie up with an old man who was slightly touched in the head. Soon he drifted asleep.

Before the rosy tinge of dawn touched the eastern sky, Fargo and the warrior were up. Fargo drank a single cup of coffee, then saddled the Ovaro. He found that Beaver Tail had cleaned both of the rifles while he was delirious with fever and learned the warrior had rubbed down the stallion every day. Usually skittish around strangers, the pinto had taken to the old man like a duck to water. He was mildly jealous.

They rode to the prairie and bore to the south. Within two hours they came on the still visible tracks made by Snake Haddock and company. There had been no heavy rain since that last great storm, so they were able to read the prints with ease.

Fargo maintained a fast pace and was surprised Beaver Tail's old war pony had no trouble keeping up with the stallion. They stopped only once, at midday to rest and water the horses in a creek. Then they galloped on. Supper consisted of a rabbit Beaver Tail dropped with an arrow. Both of them retired shortly after sunset.

Over the next six days the pattern repeated itself. Beaver Tail proved to be a chatterbox. He told Fargo not only the entire history of the Shoshoni nation, but the whole history of the world since the beginning of time as understood by his people. He also taught the Trailsman a number of Shoshoni words.

Fargo's strength increased daily. At the end of the first day he was so worn out he nearly dozed off in the saddle a few times before they called a halt. By the end of the second day his stamina was much better. After six days he was his old self, his muscles humming with power and his usual tireless energy.

During the noontime breaks he practiced with his Colt, keeping his hand in practice for the fight to come. The first such time Beaver Tail had watched him draw and break five short sticks he had stuck in the grass twenty yards off, shooting so quickly the shots blended into one report. The Shoshoni had looked solemnly at him and said, "You have the wrong name, Skye Fargo. You should be called Lightning Hands. That will be your Shoshoni name. From now on I will use only it."

On the seventh day they reached a point where the trail stopped meandering along the edge of the foothills and cut sharply to the southwest, into the dense forest. Not an hour later Fargo came on a large clearing beside a stream and was delighted to find that the outlaws had camped there two or three days, by the looks of things.

"We will gain on them now," Beaver Tail said.

Gain they did. After Haddock's gang had left the clearing, the outlaws had held their mounts to a walk, judging by the shallow hoof prints, for better than five miles, then Haddock had turned to the southwest once again. In the distance reared rugged mountains, an offshoot of the main branch of the majestic Rockies, an isolated pocket of peaks Fargo had never visited.

The trail led through thick woodland. Eventually they came to a large valley lush with thick grass and dotted with stands of trees. In turn, the valley brought them to the base of one of the unknown mountains, ending at the bottom of a high, sheer cliff. The ground was harder than ever, solid rock in some places, and tracking became increasingly difficult.

"I do not like this place," Beaver Tail commented as the shadow of the cliff engulfed them. "There is bad medicine here."

"You can ride back any time you want," Fargo said.

"Without counting coup? I am not the cowardly type who runs at the first sign of danger. You are stuck with me for a while yet."

Ahead reared a snowcapped peak. The cliff seemed to extend right up to the slope, but as they drew closer Fargo saw an opening that broadened out into the mouth of a ravine. In the dusty earth were the prints left by the Haddock gang.

"They went in here," Beaver Tail stated, his alert gaze roaming over the ravine walls. "It is a good spot for an ambush."

That it was. The walls were thirty feet apart, the floor bare of boulders and rocks. There was nowhere to take cover. A rifleman on either rim could hold off an army if need be.

Fargo shucked the Sharps and fed in a bullet. "Wait until I've gone ten yards or so, then follow. If we're bunched up it'll be easier for them to pick us off."

"Do you want me to become invisible? They might hold their fire if the see only one man and try to take you alive."

"Sure," Fargo said with a grin. "You want to turn invisible, go right ahead." He advanced into the ravine, the reins in his left hand, the rifle stock resting on his right thigh. Trying not to think of how vulnerable he was, he scanned both rims, seeking a glimmer of sunlight that would warn him an outlaw was perched above.

The ravine ran straight for fifty yards, then curved to the north. He stopped at the curve to check what lay ahead and discovered the ravine resembled a snake from there on, twisting and turning every which way as such erosion formed chasms often did. Placing his finger on the trigger of the Sharps, he glanced over his shoulder to see whether Beaver Tail was keeping the proper distance between them.

The Shoshoni was gone.

Puzzled, Fargo stared at the ravine mouth. Had the

old brave decided to return to his village after all? Or was Beaver Tail hiding near the entrance, waiting for him to return? Of one thing Fargo was positive; the warrior sure as blazes hadn't turned invisible. Shrugging, he went on. He'd rather tangle with the Haddock bunch alone, so things had worked out for the best.

The Ovaro's hoofs clopped dully on the packed earth. Since the suns rays couldn't penetrate to the bottom, the air was cool and musty.

Occasionally he saw tracks. Not clearly defined, but enough traces to reveal a large group of riders had passed into the ravine but none had come out. He wended ever farther into the recesses of the gigantic rift. Although he knew better, he relaxed slightly. So he was taken off-guard when he rounded a bend and saw a Cheyenne warrior coming the other way, painted for war and carrying a new rifle.

11

Although he was taken by surprise, Fargo's reflexes were equal to the occasion. The instant he laid eyes on the Cheyenne, he started to level the Sharps, his thumb jerking back the hammer before the rifle stopped moving. He was on the verge of firing when the warrior did something totally unexpected.

The Cheyenne used sign language, holding his right hand in front of his neck, the palm outward, the index and second fingers extending upward, and then he raised his hand until the tips of his extended fingers were as high as the top of his head. This was the sign "friend."

Perplexed, Fargo held his fire.

"I am one of Minio's band," the Cheyenne went on in sign language. "You must be one of Snake's men. They did not tell me more of you would be coming."

While the Cheyenne gestured, he came closer and closer. Fargo knew he'd had a stroke of luck, knew that it hadn't occurred to the warrior an enemy might be on Haddock's trail. He plastered a friendly smile on his face, waited until the Cheyenne was abreast of him, then swung the Sharps and rammed the stock into the brave's face, twisting his body as he swung to lend added force to the blow.

Caught unawares, the Cheyenne was slammed from his mount and landed on his back, dazed. His rifle fell to one side as he dropped. Blinking rapidly, he pushed up on his palms, then grabbed at a large hunting knife on his left hip.

Fargo beat him to the punch. His right hand had already slipped into his boot and grasped the Arkansas toothpick. He had no idea how close the outlaws and the rest of Minio's band were, so he dared not fire a shot and possibly alert them. He must kill silently, and in that respect the throwing knife was ideal. His arm arced overhead. Then, in a practiced toss he had executed countless times, he hurled the blade into the Cheyenne's chest at the precise spot necessary to pierce the heart. The entire movement, from the moment he grabbed the knife to the moment it flew from his fingers, took but seconds.

Gaping in astonishment, the Cheyenne forgot about drawing his own knife and clutched at the hilt of the toothpick. He attempted to tug it out. Failing, he opened his mouth to cry out, but instead blood gushed over his lower lip, he stiffened, and collapsed.

"Well done, Lightning Hands."

Startled, Fargo turned and saw Beaver Tail smiling at him. "Where the hell did you come from?" he growled, annoyed the old warrior had come up on him without him hearing.

"I have been here the whole time, invisible."

"Sure you have," Fargo said, suspecting the Shoshoni had secretly trailed him into the ravine and waited for just the right moment to appear as if by magic. A few years back he'd run into a medicine man who resorted to trickery to convince those in the man's tribe that he possessed supernatural abilities. Beaver Tail must be doing the same thing.

"You do not believe me?"

Fargo glanced in the direction the Cheyenne came from. "We'll talk about this later," he said, concerned another warrior or some of Haddock's men might show up. "Right now I want you to take this brave and his horse out of the ravine. Find somewhere to stash the body and let the horse go."

"What will you be doing?"

"I'll see if I can find their camp," Fargo said, glad for the excuse to go on alone. Now that he knew they were closing in, he wanted more than ever to spare Beaver Tail from harm if he could. Dismounting, he reclaimed the toothpick.

"Very well," Beaver Tail said, but he did not sound pleased. "I will catch up with you as soon as I can."

Nodding, Fargo climbed on the Ovaro and continued. At the next bend he looked back and saw that Beaver

Tail had lifted the dead Cheyenne and draped the body over the man's horse. For an oldster, the Shoshoni was quite strong.

Ten minutes of winding along brought a surprise. Suddenly the ravine widened, and before his marveling gaze stretched a pristine valley bisected by a wide stream running from west to east. On all sides towered formidable mountains, their crowns glistening white with snow. Cut off so effectively from the outside world as it was, the valley offered an ideal hiding place for renegade Indians and outlaws alike.

He remained in the shadows, surveying the sanctuary. The valley was two miles long. Half that distance off lay a tract of forest, and from near it rose a column of smoke. Waiting until certain there was no one nearby keeping a watch on the ravine, he cautiously rode out to the closest cluster of trees. By working his way from cover to cover, he worked around to the west of the smoke until he drew rein in heavy brush not two hundred yards from a small cabin. Near the cabin sat a tipi.

This was totally unexpected. A permanent building meant Snake Haddock must often retire to the valley to elude lawmen, perhaps after every robbery. The lodge indicated that not only was Minio a welcome visitor, but the Cheyenne intended to stay awhile.

His curiosity was fully aroused. What could have brought the two wicked killers together? What dirty scheme were Haddock and Minio hatching here in their hidden retreat? Whatever it was, they had to be stopped and he was just the man to handle the chore.

Fargo eased to the ground, tied the reins to a branch, yanked out his Sharps, and edged as far forward as he could without exposing himself. He spied tethered horses, both those belonging to the outlaws and three war ponies distinguished by the red symbols painted on their necks and flanks. Two renegades were outside the lodge, conversing. Three outlaws idled in front of the cabin. Nowhere did he see Snake Haddock or the women. Were Connie, Aggie, and Sophia still alive? he wondered.

Flattening, he settled down to wait until the women showed themselves or darkness fell, whichever occurred first. If he saw no trace of them before nightfall, he would sneak up to the cabin and try to learn their fate.

The afternoon waxed and waned. A sluggish breeze from the northwest barely fanned the grass. Insects buzzed, birds chirped, and squirrels argued back and forth. The natural tranquility of the scene belied the presence of the evil bands of whites and Indians notorious for the turmoil and death they caused wherever they went.

The smoke, Fargo had early noticed, came from the cabin. Every so often one of the outlaws would go in and come back out carrying a cup, probably coffee. A fourth outlaw joined them periodically. It was Porter. But where was Haddock? He got his answer as the sun perched above the mountains to the west.

Snake Haddock strolled out the front door, joked with his men, then stretched. He looked toward the tipi, cupped his hands to his mouth, and gave a shout that carried faintly to Fargo's ears. "Minio! Ain't you had enough yet? Hell, you won't be able to ride for a week if you don't take it easy." All the outlaws cackled.

Shortly thereafter a stocky Indian strode from the lodge, adjusting his buckskin shirt around his waist. He glanced at the outlaws and said something that made them all laugh the harder.

So that was the infamous Minio? Fargo mused. He sighted on the Cheyenne's torso and imagined how easy it would be to spare a lot of innocents from misery and mutilation by a simple squeeze of the trigger. Then someone else came out of the tipi, and he raised his head to see better.

It was Agatha, and she was smoothing her dress. She faced the cabin, speaking angrily and jabbing her finger at Snake Haddock for emphasis. Haddock smiled and replied, the words too low to be heard.

Fargo wished he could get closer. The next cover was a small group of pines forty yards to the northeast. Reaching them without being seen would be impossible so he reluctantly stayed put for the moment.

Sophia Jennings sashayed out of the cabin and up to Snake. She leaned against him and he draped an arm around her shoulders. This brought an angry tirade from Aggie, who might have gone on indefinitely in the same irate vein had not Minio whirled on her and slapped her full across the face. Aggie sank to her knees, a hand to her cheek.

Fargo saw Sophia start toward her and saw Snake jerk Sophia back. Minio grabbed Aggie by the hair to get her undivided attention and gave her a tongue lashing. Although Fargo couldn't make out many of the words, he determined the Cheyenne was speaking English. He watched as Minio shoved Aggie into the lodge and joined the outlaws. Everyone then went into the cabin, even the two other warriors.

All became quiet.

So now Fargo knew two of the women were alive. But what about Connie? Had Snake killed her? He saw smoke curl from the lodge and gathered that Aggie was preparing Minio's supper. Snake must have sold her or traded her to the renegade. Knowing her as he did, he doubted she would long stand for being treated as Minio's sexual plaything and domestic slave. The wild sex might be to her liking, but she would only be able to take so much of waiting hand and foot on her new master. In many tribes, the Cheyennes among them, the men ruled the roost, often with an iron hand. Whatever they wanted, the women must do. And Minio being worse than most, he was bound to push Aggie too far and turn his back on her at the wrong time. Fargo was surprised that Haddock had given her to an ally. It was the same as giving a coiled rattlesnake to someone. Only she was more dangerous.

His thinking was disrupted by the reappearance of Aggie at the tipi entrance. She looked at the cabin, then turned and beckoned for someone in the lodge to come out. Moments later someone did.

Connie.

Fargo's pulse quickened in relief at finding her alive. From the way she was holding her hands, he deduced her wrists must be bound. As she stepped farther out, he saw a rope was looped around her neck and that Aggie held the other end! What the hell was this? Connie and Aggie walked side by side around the tipi until they were screened from the cabin, then they halted and took to talking, their heads so close together they must be whispering.

He almost stood up and waved to let Connie know he was there. It was well he didn't. For out of the cabin came Minio and the two warriors, all three of them striding toward the lodge. Minio stopped and cocked his head as if he had heard the women. He motioned, and the two braves fanned out, one to the right, the other to the left.

Connie and Aggie had turned to the north and were heading for the horses when one of the braves barred their route. They spun, only to be confronted by Minio and the second warrior. Minio was beside himself. He attacked Aggie, raining punches on her shoulders and head until she was lying in the grass at his feet. Connie tried to intervene and was also knocked to the ground. At a word from Minio the other Cheyennes each grabbed one of the women and took them into the tipi.

So much had happened, so fast, that Fargo didn't know quite what to make of it all. Why was Connie with Minio? Had Haddock also handed her over to the bastard? If so, why was Connie being treated like a virtual prisoner while Aggie apparently had a free rein? Sophia being with Haddock he could understand; Snake had flat out admitted he liked her.

Fargo became uncommonly impatient for the sun to set. First he rested his chin in his left hand, then in his right. He drummed his fingers. He fidgeted. He twirled the fringe on his buckskin. Twilight shrouded the hidden valley at long last and he rose to his knees.

"I hope you are not thinking of fighting these men in your condition."

At the first whispered syllable, Fargo whirled, his right hand streaking to the Colt. The grinning countenance of Beaver Tail was so close he could reach out and touch it. "Damn!" he blurted. "Will you quit doing this?"

"Doing what?"

"Nothing," Fargo grumbled. "How long have you been here?"

"Two hours, maybe more."

Fargo couldn't believe it. Even if the crafty old devil was as quiet as a mouse, he should have *sensed* the Shoshoni's proximity. Men living in the wild often developed such an inexplicable sixth sense about such things, and his was honed to a fine degree.

"I have been invisible," Beaver Tail added.

"You took care of the body?"

"As you wanted," Beaver Tail answered. "I gave the

horse a swat on the backside, and the last I saw it was heading toward the plains. My own horse is tied next to yours."

Again was Fargo amazed. Ordinarily the Ovaro would have whinnied to let him know someone was approaching. Yet the old man came and went as he pleased without arousing the least bit alarm. How was Beaver Tail able to pull off these stunts?

"Of course," the Shoshoni said softly, "your horse did not see me because—"

"I know. I know. You were invisible," Fargo interrupted curtly. He nodded at the cabin and the lodge. "Well, now that you're here you can keep an eye on the horses while I go after Constance Jennings."

"In your condition?"

"Why do you keep saying that? There's nothing wrong with me."

"I saw you. You were as nervous as a young warrior standing under a blanket with a maiden for the very first time. I did not realize you are like those whites who can not stay still for long without acting as if they are being eaten by ants."

"I'm worried about Connie," Fargo explained. "If you saw what happened, you'd know why."

"I saw," Beaver Tail said somberly. "Minio is as bad as they say." He hefted the rifle he now held, the one that had belonged to the Cheyenne slain in the ravine. "It would be wiser if I go to check on the women. All I need do is become invisible, and the renegades and whites will have no idea someone is among them."

"Listen," Fargo said, leaning forward, "I like you, Beaver Tail, but I'm getting sick and tired of hearing about how you can turn invisible. It's just not possible. We both know it, so stop the playacting."

The Shoshoni recoiled, then said indignantly, "And I thought you were different from most whites! I should have known no white man will ever understand the ways of the spirit world. You are all dead inside." He turned and moved off, bent at the waist. "Go ahead and be killed, Lightning Hands," he whispered over his shoulder. "I know when I am not wanted."

"Wait," Fargo said, but it was no use. The old man vanished in the brush. He wasn't going to waste time going after him. The testy old cuss could get by on his own. Besides, it was now dark enough to do what had to be done.

Rotating, Fargo gripped the Sharps in his left hand and moved toward the dwellings, snaking along on his hands and knees. Stopping often to look and listen, he drew within twenty yards of the tipi. The breeze was blowing from the horses to him so he wasn't worried about one of the war ponies giving him away. From the cabin came loud voices and rough laughter. From the lodge only smoke issued.

An outlaw's mount gave a low whinny.

Fargo glanced at the string. The horse was gazing to the northwest, not at him. As he watched, it lowered its head and nibbled at some grass. Satisfied he had not been seen, he advanced. When ten yards from the tipi he heard low voices, the familiar tones of Aggie and a rough voice that could be only the renegade Minio.

Inch by inch, he worked his way to the side of the lodge and lay still, his ear nearly touching the buffalo hide. The voices were now clear.

"—should he have all that gold and you have none? There are only five of them. You and your bucks could do it and not get a scratch," Agatha was saying.

Minio grunted, and when he spoke it sounded as if his mouth was crammed full of food. "You try trick me, white bitch. I no care for gold. I no fight Snake Haddock. He friend."

"Friend, my ass. He uses you to suit his own purpose. Can't you see that?"

"No."

"Fool! You're the one who takes all the risks. You keep your eyes and ears open as you go around visiting the forts and towns. You tell him all the gossip and rumors you hear. You find out which white men are rich, which ones are right for the plucking. You let him know when valuables are being transported, like you did awhile back with that box of gold, so he can steal them. You give him important information and what do you get in return? A stinking place to hide out. That's hardly fair. You deserve more."

Fargo had listened with interest. The information explained a lot. Haddock was using the renegades as spies, a clever ploy since friendly Indians often visited forts and towns to trade or buy items, such as blankets and beads and steel knives, they could not get anywhere else. There were always Indians hanging around military posts, many who had fallen under the influence of the white man's liquor and who lived as beggars, grateful for any handouts they received. Since no one had a reliable description of Minio, it would be easy for the renegade to mingle with such hangers-on and ply them with questions about activities at the forts. Gossip spread fast on the frontier, where men had little else to entertain themselves. A careless officer, perhaps having had one too many drinks, might make a remark about an upcoming operation that would soon make the rounds of all the men and eventually be spread among everyone on the post. He heard Minio curse in Cheyenne and paid attention again.

"You try trick me, woman. You try turn me against Snake. I maybe beat you again. Beat you until you learn lesson." He repeated his words in his own tongue, and there was gruff laughter from the other two renegades.

"I learned my lesson, lover," Aggie responded calmly. "Believe you me. I won't ever be stupid enough to cross you again."

"Good."

"But I still say—"

"Enough!" Minio roared. "I no care for gold. I no fight Snake. Why you think I give him things we take from those we kill? Say words one more time, I kick your teeth out."

So there was another piece to the puzzle, Fargo reflected. When Minio struck isolated ranches and farms, he took what valuables he could find and turned them over to Snake. Since Minio always burned the homesteads to the ground, no one ever knew he was stealing as well as butchering. The arrangement was perfect. But how in the world had Snake and Minio ever joined forces? Minio supposedly hated *all* whites. Someone inside cleared their throat, and unexpectedly Connie spoke.

"May I say something?"

"What you want?" Minio responded harshly.

"You still haven't told me what you intend to do with me. I feel I have a right to know."

Minio made no reply. There were loud chewing sounds, then someone belched.

"What harm can it do in telling me?" Connie persisted. "You've hinted that you intend to sell me. But to whom?"

"What difference it make?" Minio snapped. "You bring me many horses. That all that matters."

There was a long silence broken only by the sounds of warriors eating.

"You not bad cook," Minio said at length. "Not good enough yet, but you learn."

"I've never had complaints," Aggie said.

"You cook white man's way. Need cook Indian way," Minio said. "Need know how Indian do things for you to live."

"Are you saying you'll kill me if I don't make your lousy food the way you want?" Aggie indignantly demanded.

"If you do bad again like today, I kill you. If you not obey always, I kill you. If you talk back, I kill you." Minio's voice rose. "Do anything I not like, I kill you!"

Fargo could imagine how Aggie must be boiling inside. He was surprised she hadn't taken care of Minio already. There were the other two warriors to contend with, so perhaps she was just biding her time until the right chance came along.

"We smoke pipe now," Minio announced. "You women. You not smoke. Go there with sister and not bother us."

"Yes, my lord and master," Aggie said venomously.

Rustling noises and soft footsteps sounded. Fargo realized the sisters were sitting down on the other side of the hide in front of him. They began whispering, and he had to strain to hear their words.

"I'm sorry, Connie. You were right. I should have cut you loose and let you make a run for it," Aggie said.

"You did what you thought was right. With a little luck we would have reached the horses. If the others saw you walking me around, they might have thought you were just letting me get some fresh air. Only Minio would have known differently."

"That rotten son of a bitch. I aim to deal with him soon, you can count on that. He won't tell us, but I figure he plans to sell you to the Blackfeet. And there's no way I'll let him sell kin of mine to those filthy savages." Aggie paused. "After what Sophia has done, she should be the one he sells."

"Don't talk like that. She's your sister, too."

"Some sister. She stood there and did nothing when Snake sold us to this vermin. And for what? Two stinking buffalo robes."

"I think that was Snake's idea of a joke."

Aggie replied, but Fargo didn't hear what she said. His head shot up, and he twisted to the right because distinct on the cool night air came heavy footfalls as someone approached the tipi from the cabin.

12

"Minio!" Snake Haddock bellowed. "Come out here a minute."

The outlaw was hidden from Fargo's view by the side of the lodge. He did see Haddock's shadow when the front flap was thrown open and light from the fire within bathed Snake in its glow. Clutching the Sharps to his chest, he slid as near to the lodge as he dared. Seconds passed, and suddenly the outlaw leader and Minio stepped into sight and halted. Neither gazed in his direction. Snake had his arm over Minio's shoulders.

"Has Two Bears come back yet?"

"No," Minio answered.

"I don't like it. He should have returned by now if there was nothing to find," Snake said, lowering his arm. "Maybe at first light you should ride out and see what's happened to him."

"Why you worry? Who this man who follow you?"

"He *might* be trailing us," Snake said. "There's been no sign of him but I'm not the type to take chances. Burnett and the two men I sent to rub out the son of a bitch never came back."

"Who this man?" the renegade repeated. "Why you not tell me?"

Snake stared up at the stars and sighed. "His name is Skye Fargo. Most folks know him as the Trailsman. Ever heard of him?"

"Yes. Him bad medicine. Him kill many Indians."

"And a lot of white men, too. Mostly men like me," Snake said. "Listen, I know this is a lot to ask. But we have a damn good thing going here, and I'd hate to see it come to an end. I tried to kill him and he got away. You and your braves are better than my boys when it comes to tracking and whatnot. Do me a favor and backtrack my trail. If you run into Fargo, carve him up."

"What I get?"

Snake pondered for a few seconds, then whispered, "How about if I give you the third woman when you get back? Then you can do as you please with all three."

"Thought you like her?"

"I do," Snake said and shrugged. "But a man can't ever let love stand in the way of doing business. Besides, I have me an old lady down in Santa Fe. If she ever heard about all the fooling around I do with Sophia, she'd hire someone to hunt me down and cut off my balls."

"I take her when I come back," Minio stated.

"Thanks, partner."

Fargo watched them step toward the entrance. The darkness cloaked him so well that neither had caught a glimpse of him. With two quick shots he could have slain both men, but then he would have had to deal with the rest of the outlaws and renegades all at once. And it would have been impossible to get Connie and her sisters out of there. He'd rather see the women reach a point of safety first before he settled accounts with Snake Haddock and company. The thought made him grin. Despite all that Aggie had done to him, here he was thinking about saving her. Sophia, too. He might as well face facts. Deep down he wasn't as hard an hombre as he liked to think he was. Small wonder, then, he was always getting head deep in trouble.

Haddock headed for the cabin. Minio went into the tipi and closed the flap. Skye crossed his forearms and rested his chin on them. Like any good hunter, he possessed the patience of a cougar. He would wait until everyone retired, until the renegades were sound asleep, and try to free Connie and Aggie. Sophia would have to wait.

Over two hours went by. The women whispered about the death of their father and other matters. The renegades smoked and talked in their own tongue. It was Minio who announced everyone should turn in, and it was then Aggie made a statement that brought Fargo to his knees in expectation.

"We have to go first."

"Go?" Minio said.

"Yes. Heed nature's call. Do our private business." She adopted a scathing tone. "Squaws probably don't care where or when they do it, but white women like to have some privacy."

"You go here in pot."

"Like hell we will," Aggie said. "We're not animals like some people I could mention."

Something clattered to the ground. Then there was the sound of a slap.

"Never talk that way again!" Minio fumed. "I kill next time. You understand?"

Fargo had started to back toward the rear of the lodge, but he stopped, his hope that the women would be allowed to come outside dashed. Rescuing them would be a simple matter if they did.

"Please, Minio." This was from Connie. "I know you think we are less than dogs. But is it right for you to treat us worse than you would a woman from your own tribe?"

Another slap was her answer. The renegade hissed and barked a string of words in Cheyenne. He then told the women, "I tired of talk, talk, talk! Red Hawk take both you out. If I lucky, grizzly find you! Get out my sight!"

Spinning, Fargo dashed for the closest trees. The horses were tethered nearby, and nearly every one looked up at his approach. One whinnied, but by then he was diving into the undergrowth and whirling to see if anyone had spotted him. There was no one outside the cabin. And the women and their escort had not yet appeared.

He could tell that the front flap was again thrown open because light spilled out over the grass in front of the lodge. Aggie and Connie stepped around the tipi, walking toward the trees in which he was concealed. Behind them came a tall Cheyenne armed with a rifle and a tomahawk, the latter wedged under the leather drawstring at his waist. Connie, he noticed, still had her hands bound, but the rope about her neck had been removed.

Lying on his stomach, Fargo set the Sharps to one side and brought his right knee up to his chest so he could reach into his boot for the toothpick. His eyes, because he had been outside since sunset, were well adjusted to the dark. Those of the Cheyenne and the women, however, because they had just emerged from a well-lit lodge, would take a minute or two to adjust, a fact he was counting on to give him an edge. Once the escort was close to the trees, he would pounce.

Aggie suddenly halted and faced the renegade. "My sister needs to have her hands untied."

The warrior gestured for them to keep going.

"Don't you savvy any English at all?" Aggie asked. "You must cut my sister loose."

Again the warrior gestured, this time touching his hand to his tomahawk to stress his point.

"Lousy, stinking, sons of bitches!" Aggie muttered, taking Connie's arm. They did as the Cheyenne wanted.

"Indians?" Connie asked.

"Men!" Agatha responded. "Red or white, there isn't a one of them worth a tinker's damn. They think they have the God-given right to boss women around any time they feel like it! Every last one of the bastards should be castrated."

"Oh? And what would you do to pass the time at night?"

Aggie broke stride, glanced at her sister, and laughed. "Ain't you the wonder! All that's happened to us and you still have a sense of humor? You have more grit than I ever figured, Connie, and I'm sorry I've always treated you like dirt."

Fargo eased into a crouch. The women were almost to the trees but four yards to his left. Red Hawk had relaxed his guard and had both hands at his sides. Aggie and Connie reached the first pine and halted, both of them glancing at the cabin when someone inside laughed uproariously. The Cheyenne did the same, and in that moment his back was to the Trailsman.

In a burst of movement, Fargo shot out from under cover and leaped, his arms outstretched, the blade glinting dully in his right hand. He intended to bear the warrior to the ground and dispatch him with a single well-placed thrust, but that was not to be. The Cheyenne heard him and whirled, or tried to, and got halfway around at the moment of impact. In turning, the brave brought his rifle up to chest height. So when Fargo rammed into him, the rifle was between them and the barrel deflected the toothpick.

Both men went down, the Cheyenne losing the rifle but drawing his tomahawk.

Fargo scrambled upright and slashed, anxious to end the fight quickly before the outlaws or the rest of the renegades realized what was happening. Vaguely he was aware that Aggie and Connie were running to the horses. Then the Cheyenne vented a war whoop while swinging the tomahawk.

The keen edge swished past Fargo's face and narrowly missed his shoulder. In the instant that the warrior was overextended, Fargo stabbed, plunging the blade into the man's chest. Yipping like a coyote, the Cheyenne backpedaled and pressed a hand to the spurting wound.

From the cabin and the tipi came startled yells.

So much for stealth, Fargo reflected and palmed the Colt. The revolver boomed once, the Cheyenne flipped backward, and Fargo dashed for the trees, jamming the knife under his belt as he ran. He found the Sharps and spun to see Haddock and the outlaws at the corner of the cabin while from around the front of the lodge came Minio and the other renegade. Connie, assisted by her sister, had mounted, but Aggie was having a hard time with a skittish horse.

He darted into the open again and heard one of the outlaws shout his name. Minio and the last Cheyenne disappeared in front of the tipi, but Haddock started to lead his men in a charge. Fargo fired the Colt, aiming high because he saw Sophia with the outlaws and he didn't want to hit her. Haddock and his bunch promptly sought cover.

"Fargo, come on! Move your ass!"

The urging from Aggie brought him to the horses on the fly. He vaulted onto the back of Haddock's animal, jerked the rope loose that prevented it from straying, and moved alongside the women. "Head due west!" he directed, jabbing the Sharps in the right direction, and as they took off he aimed the Colt skyward, screeched like a Comanche on the warpath, and squeezed off three shots. Half of the horses tore loose and ran. Gunfire from the cabin made him forget about trying to spook the rest of the animals. Hunching low, he rode after the sisters and overtook them shy of the heavy brush where the Ovaro waited. "Hold up!" he cried.

"What is it?" Aggie asked.

Without bothering to answer, Fargo jumped down, ran into the brush, and swung onto the stallion. The Colt went into his holster, the Sharps into its scabbard. He swiftly rejoined the women. "They'll be after us as soon as they collect their horses," he said and realized Connie's hands were still tied. Drawing the toothpick, he moved the stallion next to her mount and motioned for her to hold out her arms.

Angry shouts and curses came from the vicinity of the cabin.

"Where did you come from?" Aggie asked. "How the hell did you find us?"

"We'll talk later," Fargo said, slicing the rope carefully so as not to nick Connie's skin. She had yet to say anything, although her grateful gaze fixed on his face conveyed a world of meaning. The knife went into his boot, then he gripped the reins and motioned for them to follow. Bringing the stallion to a gallop, he headed due south for the ravine. So far as he knew it was the only way out of the hidden valley, and if the outlaws got there first they could cut off any escape. He idly wondered what had happened to Beaver Tail and hoped the Shoshoni was long gone.

A quarter of a mile from the ravine he reined up in consternation on spying a light near the entrance. It was a fire! Somehow, some of the outlaws must have gotten there already and built the blaze so that no one could get near the ravine without being spotted. Furious, he turned west again.

"Do you know what you're doing?" Aggie wanted to know.

"They have the only way of escape blocked off," Fargo answered.

"We can fight our way through."

"They'd pick us off like sitting ducks," Fargo said, slowing. To the east arose the drumming of many hoofs. Looking back, he could barely distinguish a group of horsemen riding hell bent for the ravine. More outlaws and the renegades he thought, glad none of them had spotted the sisters and him. Suddenly a rifle cracked near the fire and the horsemen scattered.

What the hell was going on? Fargo mused as he came on a gully and rode down to the bottom, then stopped. Aggie was on his left, Connie on his right. "Hold my horse," he said, flipping the reins to Connie as he pulled the Sharps and scrambled back to the top of the gully.

The outlaws were pouring gunfire into the mouth of the ravine, the bright flashes from their guns resembling oversized fireflies. If the mystery rifleman was still there, he gave no evidence of it. No more rifle shots sounded, and soon the killers got up the courage to approach the fire.

Fargo counted five men, all outlaws by the clothes and hats they wore. The biggest one had to be Snake Haddock. Where was Minio and the last renegade? Back at the cabin guarding Sophia? Sliding down, he stepped to the pinto and climbed into the saddle.

"What in the world is happening?" Aggie inquired.

"Beats the hell out of me," Fargo responded, heading north up the gully. Although, truth to tell, he had a nagging suspicion he did know who the rifleman was—none other than Beaver Tail. That crazy Shoshoni must still be hanging around in the hope of counting coup. And there was nothing he could do about it. He had to save the two sisters first.

"We have to go back for Sophia," Connie abruptly declared.

Fargo looked at her. "She's on her own."

"Sophia is our sister. We can't ride off and leave her in Snake Haddock's clutches."

"It's too dangerous."

"I saw those riders. There are only a few men left at the cabin. We'll never have a better chance to rescue her."

Connie was right and Fargo knew she was, but he glared at her anyway for being so damn logical.

"If you don't want to risk your hide, Connie and I will get her out," Aggie said.

"I'm the one who has to go in after her and you know it," Fargo grumbled. He reached the end of the gully and angled to the northeast, holding the stallion to a trot. His mind raced ahead, working on the best way to do what had to be done. Most likely, Sophia would be in the cabin. But where would the renegades be? That was the crucial question.

He changed direction, bearing to the northwest, swinging well wide of the cabin and the lodge and then coming in on them from the north. Light glowed in the sole window. Otherwise there was no sign of life. Halting under a fir tree seventy yards from the cabin, he again gave the reins to Constance. He also gave her the Sharps that had belonged to Harvey Stone and the leather ammo pouch he'd taken after shooting Murdock. His own Sharps was in his right hand as, after giving a curt nod, he moved forward.

A shadow flitted across the window.

Bending over, Fargo padded closer. On this side of the building there was less cover. He had to freeze every ten feet to listen and probe the shadows around the cabin. Nothing moved. When he was within twenty feet he went prone. Finally he heard something but not what he expected.

Now he could see Sophia pacing back and forth, bawling like a baby. He frowned. The sound of her crying would drown out more important sounds, like those made when a man moved or shifted position. If there was a Cheyenne nearby, he might not hear the warrior until too late. And he had to make his move soon. There was no telling when the outlaws would come back.

Fargo let a minute go by, then he rose and crept to the cabin. His back to the wall, he slid below the window. Sophia blubbered and wailed so loud he could scarcely hear himself think. Uncoiling, he tried to peer inside, but the blanket completely blocked off the interior.

A renegade hurtled at him from out of the gloom.

There was no telltale noise, no advance warning whatsoever, but Fargo sensed the attack an instant before the warrior reached him and spun. A fist rammed into his stomach. A knife flashed past his face and struck the log behind his head. Stunned, he nonetheless lashed out, kicking the Cheyenne in the shin and driving the rifle stock into the renegade's forehead. The Indian hardly seemed fazed. A hand clutched the rifle barrel, and then they were toppling to one side.

Fargo twisted his head aside as the knife streaked at his neck. He had no choice but to release the Sharps and grab the warrior's knife arm. The Cheyenne's other hand clamped on his throat and squeezed. They struggled savagely, rolling over and over. Fargo tried to pry the renegade's fingers from his throat, but they were like iron bands. And all the while, in the back of his mind, he worried about Minio, who must be close at hand.

A knee slammed into his thigh, missing his groin by an inch. Enraged, Fargo whipped his forehead into the warrior's face. Cartilage crunched. Blood sprayed from the Cheyenne's crushed nose. For a second the brave's grip slackened, and Fargo capitalized by wrenching the man's hand from his neck. His own hand flew to his Colt, and he nearly had the gun out when the renegade recovered sufficiently to gouge a finger into his eye. Racked with pain, he jerked his face away, and the Cheyenne tried to gouge his other eye.

By then the Colt was clear, and Fargo jammed the barrel into the warrior's side, thumbed back the hammer, and fired. The renegade stiffened, arched his spine, and gasped, his limbs going limp. Fargo shoved him off and rose to one knee, ready to shoot again. But the Cheyenne was on his back, his mouth agape, wheezing weakly. Seconds later he stopped breathing.

Turning, Fargo scanned the area for Minio. Seeing no one, he grabbed the Sharps and ran for the front door, getting there just as Sophia threw it wide and stood framed in the doorway.

"Fargo!" she blurted.

"We're getting out of here!" Fargo said, his eyes on the tipi. He shoved the Colt into his holster, grasped her wrist, and went to run off when he saw three horses tethered north of the lodge. "Where's Minio?" he asked urgently.

"I don't rightly know. Snake ordered me to stay inside and told me one of the Injuns would make sure I stayed put. Then him and the rest hightailed it out of here."

"Go!" he said, giving her a shove northward. "Keep going until you see your sisters. Yell a lot so they'll know it's you, and wait with them until I get there."

Sophia obediently sprinted away, her dress clinging to her willowy legs.

Cocking the Sharps, Fargo jogged to the lodge. Since Haddock had told Sophia only one Indian would stand guard, Minio must be elsewhere. He yanked the flap open and crouched. A small fire crackled softly in the center. Piled along the right wall were a half-dozen rifles. At the rear was enough ammunition to outfit an army. To the left lay odds and ends, including two large parfleches and beaded rawhide pouches Indians used to carry food and other items. He inspected them and found one partially filled with venison jerky, the other with pemmican. Tucking them under his left arm, the Sharps in his left hand, he picked up a buffalo robe and held it over the fire. Perhaps he could draw Haddock away from the ravine long enough to hasten the women out of the valley.

The robe caught rapidly, flaring into flame. He dashed to the side of the tipi and pressed the robe against the hide wall until the flames were eating at the lodge itself. Then he ran outside, over to the cabin, and tossed the burning robe inside, against the front wall.

Snake Haddock was in for a surprise.

Pivoting, Fargo sped to the horses. He released two, gave a sharp yell, and they bolted into the brush. The third horse took him back to where the sisters waited. He handed the reins to Sophia, then forked leather. As he draped the parfleches over the back of his saddle, Aggie cried out.

"Look there!"

Roaring flames engulfed the tipi from top to bottom. Brilliant red and orange tendrils danced in the air. Soon the ammunition would catch. Over at the cabin, smoke poured from the doorway and flames were visible in the window.

"Ride!" Fargo roared, heading the stallion northeast. The sisters fell in behind him. They were a hundred yards from the blazing structures when the crisp mountain night reverberated with a blast that ripped the tipi to bits. "That should get Snake's attention," he said, swinging southeast.

"You fight dirty," Aggie said with a grin. "I like that in a man."

"He only does what has to be done," Connie said defensively. "Don't drag him down to your level."

"Oh, wonderful! We're not out of the frying pan yet, and she starts in on me again," Aggie said.

"Quiet, both of you!" Fargo barked. Given what Agatha had done to him, he was in no mood to listen to her prattle on about how great he was. He'd fallen into that trap before, and a man who stuck his head in the same noose twice deserved to have it torn right off. Ahead loomed forest. He glanced at the sky to get his bearings. In order for his plan to succeed, they must come out of the woods as close to the ravine as possible.

"Skye?" Sophia said apprehensively.

"What?" Fargo snapped.

"I think we're being followed."

13

Skye Fargo twisted. For a fleeting instant he thought he saw something move far behind them, but he couldn't be certain. Seconds passed, and there was no other clue as to what it might have been. Facing the trees, he led the sisters into the murky realm of indistinct shapes and shadows where they had to be on their toes at all times to avoid logs, boulders, and countless trunks and branches.

For half a mile they pressed southward, then Fargo bore to the southwest, toward the ravine. Only then did he slow down. Another check to his rear showed no trace of pursuit. Perhaps he had only imagined he saw something, but with Minio unaccounted for he wasn't taking any chances. He surveyed their back trail repeatedly until he came to a small clearing less than fifty yards from the ravine. There he drew rein.

"Why are we stopping?" Aggie whispered.

"I'm not about to ride into an ambush," Fargo responded, sliding from his saddle. "I'll go see if Haddock and his men are still there. None of you budge until I come back."

"I'm coming with you," Connie declared, firmly gripping the rifle he had given her. She started to climb down.

"You should stay to protect your sisters," Fargo said and was surprised when she disregarded his advice, dismounted, and stepped over to him.

"They can take care of themselves. They always have," Connie said bitterly. "Besides, you'll need someone to watch your back and I'm a fair shot."

Aggie snickered. "That's as good an excuse as any. Go get him, gal!"

Rather than engage in yet another argument and waste

more valuable time, Fargo hefted his Sharps, turned, and made off through the woods, gliding soundlessly on cat's feet. Connie did almost as well, occasionally snapping small twigs underfoot or rustling the vegetation. She glued herself to his heels, and he could hear her excited breathing. When he halted behind a tree and crouched, she did likewise, her shoulder brushing his.

The fire at the ravine still burned, but barely. In the dim glow two men could be seen standing a few yards in front of the entrance, their attention riveted on the distant burning cabin.

"Where are the rest?" Connie whispered in his ear, her warm breath tingling his skin.

"If they took the bait, Haddock and the other two are heading for the cabin," Fargo answered.

"You're awful clever," Connie said, smiling, her teeth white in the night. She leaned closer and gave him a soft kiss on the cheek.

"What was that for?"

"Do I need a reason?" Connie rejoined. "Very well. You saved our hash earlier, and that was my way of saying how much I appreciate all you've done for us." She kissed him once more, only this time full on the mouth. "And that was a hint of things to come if you play your cards right."

Fargo had to admit one thing about the Jennings sisters. They sure as hell picked the absolutely worst times to be romantic. He touched her chin and said softly, "If we get out of this fix, I'll take you up on your offer." Then he faced the mouth of the ravine.

The pair of outlaws, made careless by their concern over the fire, were making no effort to conceal themselves. Fargo could drop them both from where he was. But the shots would carry far, perhaps to Snake Haddock's ears, and the rest of the outlaws would race back before Fargo got the women all the way through the ravine. Once again stealth was called for.

"Stay here," Skye said, adding quickly to stifle any protest. "And this time do as you're told." Staying low, he moved into the open, swinging to the left to come at the fire from the back side. Neither outlaw so much as glanced in his direction, and he attained the east wall of the ravine without trouble. Pausing, he drew the Colt, and with the revolver in his right hand and the rifle in his left, he tiptoed up to the outlaws, placing each foot down with the utmost care, until he was so close he could have kicked them in their backsides if he wished. Instead, he touched the rifle to one man's back, the revolver to the other's, and warned, "If you want to die, make a move."

Both hard cases froze.

"I want each of you to take your six-shooter and give it a good heave," Fargo went on. "And do it slow or you'll never live to see your share of the gold."

They did as they were told.

Fargo nodded. "Thanks, boys. I hope we meet again some day so I can blow your brains out." So saying, he swung the revolver in an arc, clubbing the outlaw on the right on the back of the head. The man's knees buckled. Instantly the second outlaw tried to whirl and was struck on the temple. A second blow dropped him like a poled ox.

The first outlaw swayed and put a hand on the ground to steady himself.

"Pleasant dreams," Fargo joked, and clubbed the man again, a vicious swipe that felled him flat. Turning, Fargo dashed to the trees. "Go get your sisters and the horses," he said.

"We'll hurry," Connie promised.

He waited until she was out of sight, then went to the outlaws and dragged them out of the light. Since the cabin was a mile off, he wasn't worried about Snake or anyone else recognizing him. He passed in front of the fire several times, searching for the two horses that must be nearby. A low nicker took him right to them, secreted a dozen yards into the ravine. Neither resisted when he led them out.

The women were galloping toward him, Connie in the forefront and leading the Ovaro.

"From now on we ride like the wind," Fargo announced as they stopped. "By the time Snake realizes we've slipped through his fingers, we'll be long gone."

"This horse of yours gave me a hard time," Connie said as she handed over the stallion's reins.

"It's a contrary critter, just like its owner," Aggie commented gaily.

Fargo failed to see why she was in such good spirits, and he wasn't about to ask. They weren't out of danger yet and wouldn't be until they were miles from the ravine. Swinging up, he stuck the Sharps in the scabbard but kept the Colt in his right hand. "Aggie, you bring one of these horses. Sophia, you bring the other one," he instructed them and was pleased when neither of them objected.

Near total darkness shrouded the floor of the ravine in an inky mantle. The high walls blocked out all of the sky except for a narrow strip of stars. Fargo felt as if he was riding into the bowels of the earth and disliked the sensation of being hemmed in. He kept alert since there was a remote chance that Haddock had sent one of the gang to the other end of the ravine. His thumb resting on the Colt's hammer, he rode slowly, cocking his head to better hear any faint sounds on the sluggish air.

His eyes grew as accustomed as was humanly possible to the pitch-black conditions. Both walls were blank slates. The women and their mounts were no more than black blobs. He could hardly see the pinto's head, and he marveled that the stallion was able to pick its way along without bumping into every bend and crook in their path.

By his estimation they were about halfway through when the ravine reverberated to the booming retort of a rifle. He spotted the gun flash on the rim of the west wall a hair before the slug smacked into the right-hand wall and sent sharp slivers into his cheek and neck. Squeezing off two shots, he put his spurs to the Ovaro and shouted, "Ride, ladies! Ride!"

The rifle thundered again but was nearly drowned out in the din of drumming hoofs. Fargo heard the sisters urging their mounts on and hoped none of them would become unhorsed. Shifting, he sent two more shots at the rim. This time they went unanswered.

Fargo dared not stop. The women might not realize he had and run into him. Despite the risk of clipping a wall, he galloped along the winding ravine for what seemed like an eternity, until all of a sudden the pinto hit a straight stretch and in moments they were out in the open at the base of the towering cliff. He slowed and wheeled the Ovaro as Connie and Aggie emerged. But not Sophia. Tense seconds ensued. Then the ravine rang to the pounding of more hoofs and out she came, her long hair flying, her dress hiked up around her thighs. But the horse she had been leading was gone, and she was bent over as if in pain.

"What happened?" Fargo asked when she halted in front of him. "Were you shot?"

"My damn horse smacked into a wall when we were going around a corner," Sophia said, wincing and tentatively raising her left arm. "About broke my shoulder. I'm afraid I lost hold of that horse you told me to bring."

"Can you ride on?"

"Watch me!"

Fargo headed due east, into the valley, relishing the wind on his face and thinking ahead to when he would drop the sisters off at the nearest settlement and be on his own again. After all he had been through, a week of peace and quiet would be like heaven on earth.

"Skye," Aggie said, drawing abreast of him. "What's your rush? We should find a spot and wait for Snake to show, then put an end to him once and for all." She indicated the horse she was leading. "There's a rifle in the scabbard so we have enough guns to do the job."

"Why bother?" Fargo replied. "In ten minutes or so we'll be out of Snake's reach."

"Don't count on it. Burnett might be dead, but there's always Minio. He's an Injun so he must be a dandy tracker."

"He'll have to wait until daylight. By then we'll be miles from here."

"And what about the gold?"

Fargo glanced at her. "So that's it. You want to kill Snake and keep all the gold for yourself."

"I'll share it with you. But we can't kill him right off because he's the only one who knows where it's at."

"What?"

Aggie nodded. "He took the box shortly after we got to the cabin and went off somewhere to bury it. Wouldn't let a soul go with him and threatened to shoot any man who tried to follow. And some of them wanted to, believe me. Porter was fit to be tied. He didn't like it one bit."

"Forget the gold, Aggie. It's brought you nothing but grief."

"Are you loco? Forget about being rich? Forget about being able to buy all the fancy clothes I want and living in a big mansion with servants at my beck and call? Not on your life."

"Haven't you learned your lesson yet? You stole that box from Snake and what has it gotten you? Your pa is dead. You were forced to go to bed with a renegade—"

"That part wasn't so bad," Aggie said, grinning. "Minio is a murdering savage, but he's one of the best danged lovers I ever had."

"You'll never learn," Fargo said and sighed.

"What's to learn? If a body wants to get ahead in this world, she has to take what she wants when she wants it. I saw a golden opportunity to make my whole family as wealthy as old King Midas and I took it."

Fargo's curiosity got the better of him. "How did you swing that, by the way?"

"It was as simple as taking candy from a baby," Aggie said. "Snake and his bunch hit an army patrol down New Mexico way. The patrol was escorting a wagon carrying the gold. Snake's boys wiped them out to the last man." She giggled. "Not that it was all that hard to do after we got done with them."

Memories of Harvey Stone made Fargo frown. "How do you mean?"

"Connie, Sophia, and me were as much a part of Snake's gang as Pa. Well, Sophia and me, anyway. Connie never did cotton to doing some of the things we had to do."

"Such as?"

"Oh, things like snuggling up to fools with fat wallets and getting them good and drunk so Snake would have no trouble taking their money. We did the same with those army boys. Got most of them drunk the night before they were to leave. Sophia and me even took a couple of them to bed and kept them up all night long. I took the lieutenant, as I recollect, and she used her charms on their scout. Those poor fools were in no shape for a fight when Snake hit them."

Fargo made no comment.

"So the whole affair went off without a hitch and we

skedaddled. Snake and the men had a talk and decided to stash the box until things quieted down. That was about the time my pa figured he had ridden the outlaw trail long enough and told Snake he was calling it quits. Snake told Pa to look him up in a month and Pa would get his share of the gold."

"But you had a better idea."

"I sure did. Pa's notion about quitting set me to thinking. His share wouldn't last long. We needed more than that if we wanted to live in grand style. I don't need to tell you I'm not the kind to scrub floors for a living."

"No, you don't."

"So I stole the gold."

"You?"

Agatha laughed. "All by my lonesome. Lord, was that thing heavy! I had to tie a rope around it, throw the rope over a limb, then tie the other end to my saddle horn and use my horse to lift the box high enough to put it on one of our pack animals. Naturally I didn't tell Pa or my sisters what I had done for two days. By then we were well shed of Snake."

"How did your pa take the news you had double-crossed Haddock?"

"At first he was riled. So was Sophia. But I won them around to my way of thinking, and Pa headed for the most remote part of the country he could find so Snake wouldn't be able to find us. I wanted to go east to a big city, but he wouldn't listen to me."

"How did Connie feel?"

"I can answer that," Connie said, coming up on Fargo's other side. "I told them flat out that stealing the gold from Snake was the worst thing they could have done, that Snake would stop at nothing to get the gold back, that he'd hunt us down forever if that's what it took. And I was right." She jabbed a finger at Aggie. "Your greed got Pa killed and for that I'll never forgive you. Once we're out of this, I'm going my own way. Sophia and you are on your own."

"We're kin. We need to stick together."

"Go to hell."

Aggie stuck her nose in the **air and** sniffed. "You always have acted as if you're **too** good for us. See if I care what you do." Turning her mount, she moved back to ride with Sophia.

"I should have done this years ago," Connie said to Skye. "But I never had the courage."

Fargo altered course again, bearing southeast. They were making good time, and he planned to push their horses to the point of exhaustion. The more miles they covered before daylight, the harder it would be for Snake Haddock to catch them. Through dense forest they rode, through valleys and past regal peaks, across meadows and over hills, forging on hour after hour until a pink tinge flushed the eastern horizon. Then Fargo searched for a spot to camp.

He found an ideal location high on the side of a hill that had been scarred by a rampaging fire. Apparently lightning had struck a pine near the top of the hill, igniting the tree, and the flames then spread to the bottom of the hill where they were contained by a creek flowing from north to south. Now charred trunks and limbs were all that remained. From a distance the entire slope appeared black.

A closer inspection revealed a portion of the hill had buckled, the result of erosion caused by heavy rain after the fire, creating a wide, bowl-shaped depression eight feet high. A dirt ramp took them to the bottom of the bowl, where Fargo climbed down.

This was perfect, he realized. They would be able to see anyone approaching from far away, but no one could see them unless right on top of them. He gestured and said, "This is where we'll rest a spell."

"How long?" Sophia asked. "My shoulder is killing me. I could sleep all day long."

"Until noon," Fargo said. "Then we head for the prairie."

"Well, six hours of sleep is better than nothing," Aggie remarked, dismounting. She stretched, her full breasts straining against the fabric of her dress. Then she winked at Fargo and grinned.

Fargo, ignoring her, began going from horse to horse, taking in hand either the reins or the rope leads. Some people just never learned. Aggie was one of those with no conscience whatsoever. She did as she damn well pleased and hang the consequences. What did she care if another person got hurt along the way? All that mattered to her was herself.

"What are you doing?" Connie asked.

"Someone needs to water the horses," Fargo said.

"You can't take all these animals in one trip alone," Connie responded, quickly snatching the reins of a bay. "I'll lend you a hand."

"Someone should keep watch."

Aggie tittered. "Hell, there's no way Snake can get here any time soon. But if it will make you feel better, I'll keep my eyes peeled until you two are done."

Sophia had already sat down with her back to the side of the bowl and was vigorously rubbing her sore shoulder. "Can we start a fire? A couple of cups of coffee would do wonders right about now."

"No fire," Fargo answered, walking up the incline. "The smoke would give us away."

"Not even a small one?" Sophia pressed.

"No," Fargo said. What was left of the burnt brush crackled underfoot as he took the horses down to the creek. Below in the pines the birds were coming alive, singing gaily to greet the new day. An invigorating cool breeze from the north tingled his skin and helped him forget how tired he felt.

"Isn't the wilderness beautiful?" Connie asked, standing aside as her horses lined up to dip their muzzles in the water. She clasped her hands behind her back and gazed out over the picturesque countryside.

"I've always thought so," Fargo admitted. He looked up toward their hiding place, but the angle of the slope prevented him from seeing it. He could only hope that Aggie was keeping watch as she had promised.

"Do you live in the mountains all the time? Don't you ever miss civilization?"

"I visit towns and cities now and then," Fargo said, "but I never stay all that long." He stared at the lofty mountains to the west. "Out here a man can do as he pleases. There's no one trying to ride roughshod over him. He's as free as the wildlife and the Indians."

"And you cherish your freedom?"

"More than anything else."

"Is that why you've never married? A handsome man like you must have had lots of offers."

"There have been a few," Fargo said, grinning at the

recollections. "But I'm not ready to settle down yet. Until I am, there isn't a woman alive who will hogtie me."

"That's too bad," Connie said, sounding genuinely sad. "The woman who hooks you will be in for a happy life, I reckon."

"Thanks," Fargo said, not quite knowing what else to say and wondering why she had bothered to bring up the subject. A second later he had his answer when she put down her rifle, slowly strolled over, and looked up into his eyes.

"Do you find me attractive?"

"Sure," Fargo honestly replied, brazenly admiring her lithe figure. She wasn't as full-bodied as her sisters, but her trim figure possessed vitality and grace. Where Agatha and Sophia might be compared to thoroughbreds, Connie was a frisky young mare just coming into the prime of her sexual life.

"Then why haven't you made love to me?"

Fargo hesitated. How did a man answer a crazy question like that?

"You've been with both Aggie and Sophia," Connie continued. "I know because they've bragged about how good you are. They've even argued over which one of them you liked the best." She frowned. "It's not been easy, being raised in a family with two sisters who have one thing on their mind all the time. Sex, sex, sex. Did you know Aggie first made love when she was sixteen years old?"

"No."

Connie nodded. "And Sophia went into the wood shack with our cousin when she was even younger. I happened to walk by and heard her squealing with pleasure."

Fargo waited for what was coming.

"All my life they've had all the fun and I've been the dutiful daughter. And that's hasn't been fair. It's about time I enjoyed some of the good things life has to offer." Connie reached up and put her hands on his shoulders. "Do you want me?"

"Does a bear like honey?"

Smiling self-consciously, Connie planted her lips on his, tentatively at first, but with increasing ardor as her passion climbed. She gasped when he suddenly placed his hands on her pert breasts and squeezed. When they broke for air, she panted and said, "Oh, my! That felt good."

Fargo took her in his arms. "It gets better."

14

Fargo was convinced he had outdistanced the outlaws. He was certain Snake and the rest were just beginning their pursuit. So he had time to kill. And while sleep was in order, he was never one to say no to a willing lady. He cupped Connie's buttocks in his hands and tweaked them as his tongue darted into her silken mouth. She kissed exquisitely, her thin tongue swirling around his, her thighs grinding into his legs.

He forgot all about the horses and the birds. He forgot everything except the pleasure of holding a hot-blooded woman and feeling her body mold itself to his. She yielded completely, her legs parting to permit his right hand to slide between her thighs, and she uttered a soft cry of rapture when his fingers stroked her slit.

"I'm getting all wet!"

His lips roamed over her cheeks, her chin, her throat. He sucked on her earlobes while breathing heavily into her ears. His left hand fondled her breasts. His right caressed her womanhood. She shifted from foot to foot, squirming deliciously, nibbling on his neck.

Picking her up, he carried her to a level spot where the grass had not been burned and gently deposited her on the ground. Her hungry gaze made him hurry in removing his gun belt and loosening his pants. He sank down beside her, his mouth finding hers again, and was surprised when she slid a hand into his pants and lightly gripped his organ.

"I had no idea you were so big," she cooed, stroking him with a fingertip.

Fargo nearly exploded in his pants. Gritting his teeth, he kept the lid on and unfastened her dress to gain access to her breasts. Once they were free, he licked and kissed and massaged them. His right hand hiked the lower half of her dress up to her waist, exposing her smooth thighs and her white underthings.

"Do anything you want!" Connie whispered in his ear. "Make me forget."

Forget what? Fargo wondered, and shelved the question for future consideration. There was a time and a place for everything, and gabbing in the middle of making love was not one of them. He licked her flat stomach and nuzzled her inner thighs.

"Yesssss!" Connie said.

He pressed his lips to her crack, then inserted his tongue and wiggled it around. Instantly she bucked and locked her fingers in his hair.

"Do it, Skye! Do it!"

Resting his elbows under her bent legs, Fargo used his tongue to transform her tunnel into an inferno. His pole pulsed under the hard rubbing of her fingers. As much as he would have liked to go on indefinitely, he didn't know how much longer he could retain his self-control.

Connie removed her hand from his pants and gave him a passionate kiss, her lips moist and soft. Her hands roved over his broad chest and muscular stomach. "You make me want it so much," she huffed.

It was then that Fargo heard a dry twig snap somewhere above them. He glanced up the hill to see someone dart behind a large charred trunk. The glimpse was fleeting, no more than an impression of a shadowy figure, and he figured it must be Aggie spying on them. Anger flared, to be replaced by a crooked smile. So the bitch was watching them, was she? Good. He'd give her an eyeful she would never forget.

He dallied now, his mouth lingering at each of Connie's breasts as his hands fondled her thighs and her pubic mound. His forefinger brushed her nether lips time and again, but he did not penetrate. Her legs closed tight on his arm. The heat from her core was incredible.

Connie dug her nails into his back and arms, her breathing like that of a steam engine. "What you're doing to me!" she said.

Fargo scanned the slope again but didn't see Aggie. Maybe she had gone back to the bowl, he reasoned. It really didn't matter. He wasn't about to stop, not even if the world should come to an end. Spreading Connie's legs, he touched his pole to her slit, tensed, and thrust.

"AAAaaaaahhhh!" she groaned, clasping him tight, her face buried against his shoulder.

Ecstasy took over. The feel of Connie's glassy walls as they enveloped his organ like a living sheath brought tremors to Fargo's body. Clutching her hips, he commenced a rhythmic stroking, gradually at first, his mouth parted in rapture as she met each thrust with a counterthrust of her own. Carnal pleasure filled his every pore. His eyes half-closed, his arms corded like steel bands, he increased the force of his strokes, listening to the smack-smack-smack of their frenzied forms.

Connie opened her mouth wide, and Fargo thought for a moment she would scream her head off. But she jammed part of her dress between her lips and bit down as her body came up off the grass in wild abandon.

Fargo was close to the ultimate explosion. His organ seemed to fill her completely. He rammed into her once more, then held still for a bit, savoring the total sensuality. Without warning, Connie began churning and humping as a woman insane, her inner juices coating his manhood as she came, came, came.

"Ooooooohhhhh!"

That was the last straw. Fargo let himself go, ramming into her over and over, his whole universe reduced to the monumental explosion in his loins. His senses swam. He trembled. He shut his eyes and rode her until her arms fell away. Then he slowed and opened his eyes to see her smiling in satisfaction. Gradually he coasted to a stop and lay on top of her.

Several minutes passed before she broke the silence.

"That was terrific. You're every bit as marvelous as my sisters claimed."

"Glad I lived up to my reputation," Fargo said and kissed her.

"It's too bad you're not the marrying kind," Connie commented dreamily. "Or I'd try to throw a noose around you my own self."

They rested quietly. Lulled by the tranquility, Fargo began to doze off and jerked his head up. If he fell asleep he might not wake up until evening, allowing Haddock's bunch to overtake them. It would be embarrassing as hell to be caught with his britches down. That had happened before, and he'd vowed it would never happen again.

"We should head back," he declared, easing onto his knees.

"I suppose," Connie said reluctantly, then she brightened and laughed.

"What did I miss?"

"Nothing. I'm thinking of how much fun I'll have rubbing Aggie's nose in the fact I made love to you, too. She'll be mad as a wet hen."

"If you want to get her really riled, tell her that I liked you the best," Fargo said.

"I wouldn't want to lie."

Fargo's heart went out to this lovely young woman who had been raised in a family of cutthroats, yet who had managed to salvage her dignity from the ordeal. "It's the truth," he said softly.

Connie blinked, grinned, and hugged him. "Thank you. You have no idea how much that means to me."

They dressed in silence. Fargo finished first and gathered the horses. Connie fussed with her hair, then picked up the Sharps he had given her. His own rifle rested in his saddle scabbard as the two of them walked side by side up the slope. He thought about taking it out but the peaceful setting, combined with that contented feeling a man gets after a heated bout of frenzied lovemaking, lulled him into a sense of complacency. For a few moments in time everything was right with the world, and he enjoyed not having to be extra vigilant.

That all changed when they were a third of the way up. Fargo paused and twisted, staring at the woodland below, bothered by something he couldn't quite put his finger on.

"What is it?" Connie asked.

"I don't rightly know," Fargo confessed. But suddenly he did know. All the birds had fallen silent. They rarely did so without a reason, usually because a predator was on the prowl or a party of men was passing by. He didn't think that Connie and he had made enough noise to be responsible, so there must be another cause. But what?

Abruptly, Fargo remembered the figure he had glimpsed a short while ago. Now that his mind wasn't clouded by lust, he realized he should have gone to see who it was then and there. He headed upward, tugging on the reins and rope leads in his hand.

"Something is wrong. I can tell by your face," Connie said, nervously scouring the hill. "What?"

"I'm not sure yet," Fargo said, his uneasiness growing. The closer he got to their hiding place, the worse it became. A dozen yards away he let go of the horses and ran, his right hand closing on the Colt. He vaulted a charred log, drew the revolver, and flew up the last few feet. On the rim he halted, seeking Aggie and Sophia.

They were there, all right, lying on their backs in the dirt. Sophia's arms were out flung, her eyes wide in the astonishment she must have felt when death claimed her. Jutting from her chest was a Cheyenne arrow.

Near the center of the bowl, close to a rifle she must have tried to reach, lay Agatha. Three arrows riddled her, one in the chest and two in the back. A crimson pool rimmed her body.

"Oh, God!"

Fargo turned at Connie's horrified wail and saw the shock setting in. She moaned, tears filling her eyes. "Don't look at—" he started to say, when a hard voice to his rear cut him off.

"Want to die, white dog?"

Fargo held the Colt next to his leg. He could spin and shoot and hope to high heaven he dropped the renegade before the renegade dropped him. But Minio undoubtedly had him covered, probably with an arrow. He'd likely have a shaft in him before he completed the turn. And even if by some miracle Minio missed, the shaft might well strike Connie.

"Drop guns. Now!"

As much as Fargo wanted to kill the murderous savage, he let the Colt fall.

"Woman drop rifle. Do it!"

Transfixed by the sight of her dead sisters, Connie didn't seem to hear the command. Tears trickled down her cheeks, and she sniffled loudly.

"Now!" Minio roared.

"Allow me," Fargo said, holding his arms out from his sides so the renegade could see them clearly. Taking a step to the left to give Minio an unobstructed view of Connie, he slowly reached out and grasped the barrel of her rifle. She stood numb and unresisting as he lowered the gun to the ground.

"Turn, white dog."

Fargo complied. Not eight feet off was Minio, an arrow nocked to his bowstring, a wicked sneer curling his cruel mouth. "I reckon you're better than I figured. How did you find us this soon?"

"Follow you after you set fires," Minio replied, lowering the bow a few inches as he reduced the space between them by half. "Wait for right time."

"And now what?"

"Take you and bitch to Snake. Him maybe want you bad after what you do." Minio snickered. "He likes to kill, likes hear people scream." The Cheyenne nodded at the horses. "Get rope. Any tricks, I kill woman."

A snail could have moved faster than Fargo did. Deliberately dragging his heels to give himself time to think, he tried to come up with a way out of the fix they were in. The stock of his Sharps projecting above the Ovaro's neck was a tempting sight, and he nearly made a mad grab for it. He was confident he could slay Minio, yet at what price? Connie was the last of her family left alive, and he intended to see she stayed that way. He took a rope off of one of the horses belonging to the outlaws. Minio watched him like a hawk as he returned and held the rope out. "Here."

"Give to woman."

Fargo nudged Connie but she stood rooted in place, her features blank, her breathing shallow. "Connie," he said, and nudged her again. She uttered a pitiable whine.

"Slap her," Minio said.

"Like hell I will," Fargo responded. He placed a hand on her arm and gave her a gentle squeeze. "Connie, it's me, Skye. If you don't take this rope you're going to wind up like your sisters. Do you understand?"

She bobbed her chin once and gripped the rope limply. "Both . . . dead," she said in a daze. "All gone now." More tears poured from her red eyes.

"Tie him, bitch!" Minio barked. "Tie or I shoot him in the belly."

For the first time Connie appeared to realize the Cheyenne was there. A look of sheer hatred rippled across her face and she took a half step toward him. "You! You did this, you son of a bitch!"

Minio wagged his bow. "One more word and this man dies. You tie hands behind his back. Do it quick or he look like porcupine."

Glaring defiantly, Connie stepped behind Fargo, joined his wrists together, and looped the rope under Minio's careful scrutiny.

Fargo held his arms rigid and a fraction of an inch apart as she tied so that when he relaxed them later there would be slack in the rope. If she noticed the ploy, she did nothing to give him away. Minio grunted when she was done, then motioned for her to step aside. Lowering his bow, he quickly stepped in close and snatched Skye's Colt. The hammer clicked as he thumbed it back.

"Now go to horses."

Fargo saw the renegade take the other end of the rope as he walked down to the Ovaro. "How am I supposed to climb up with my hands tied?" he asked.

"That you figure out or die."

It took three attempts before Fargo was able to hook his boot in the stirrup. Leaning against the stallion, he surged upward. His boot began to slip and he thought he would topple, but by bending forward he was able to swing his other leg over the pinto and right himself. He found the second stirrup without any problem. Then there was a tug on the rope.

"I hold this," Minio declared. "Any trick, I pull you off horse and slit your throat. Savvy, white dog?"

"I understand," Fargo said. He knew he shouldn't look a gift horse in the mouth, but he was puzzled. Why had Minio slain Aggie and Sophia but spared Connie and him? Was it a token gesture of friendship for Snake, or was it a another motive?

Connie mounted, and once she was up Minio did the same, swinging onto an outlaw's horse. He told her to bring the rest of the animals, and when she was under way he gave the Ovaro a slap on the rump, then fell in behind them. As they entered the forest, he halted. "Stop!"

Fargo glanced around and saw the Cheyenne give a sharp whistle. From out of the brush came a black war pony. Minio changed mounts by sliding from one horse to the other, his moccasins never touching the ground. Then he motioned and they resumed their journey.

Fatigue made Fargo slump in the saddle. He wanted nothing so much as ten hours or more of uninterrupted sleep. He also wanted the renegade to ride in front of him so he could work on the rope binding his wrists, but for the next two hours Minio stayed at the rear the whole time.

Connie looked at him a few times. It was not difficult to guess what she was thinking because her gaze invariably went past him and focused on the renegade, her eyes revealing her innermost wish. If she got half a chance, she was going to try and slay Minio.

Fargo hoped she wouldn't do anything rash before he freed himself. The Cheyenne had spared them once, for whatever reason, but he doubted Minio would be so charitable a second time. He could feel the toothpick rubbing against his ankle and longed to get his hands on it.

Then they came to a valley and he saw the dust.

A mile off, adjacent to a rugged peak, rose a small brown cloud. He recollected passing that peak the night before and seeing it silhouetted against the backdrop of stars. If so, then the dust was being raised by Haddock's bunch. And it meant the outlaws had not waited for dawn to give chase. They must have started well before daylight, using torches to hunt for tracks.

Minio laughed. "Snake want you bad, Trailsman. I bet you take long time dying."

Fargo knew he must do something quickly, before the outlaws came into sight. If he fell into Haddock's clutches it would all be over except the screaming. But what could he do with his wrists bound? Fleeing was useless. Minio would simply yank on the lariat, dumping him on the ground. Jumping Minio was an equally ridiculous idea. The renegade was too far back, for one thing, and would be as hard to take unawares as a cougar.

A few spruce were the only trees in the valley. As they were passing one, Minio reined up and called out, "We wait here. Maybe Snake want to hang you, Fargo." Grinning, he grasped the rope in both hands and jerked.

There was little Fargo could do. He tried to lock his boots in the stirrups as he fell backward, but neither caught hold. He was unable to prevent himself from tumbling headfirst to the dank earth. Pain racked his neck and spine. His lower back was severely wrenched. Rolling onto his side, he heard the renegade cackle.

"You the one Snake worry about? You the white dog who kill so many warriors?" Minio spat in disgust. "You nothing! Women of my tribe are better fighters." Climbing down, he threw the rope at his feet and approached with the Colt cocked and leveled. "Maybe I kill now, save Snake trouble."

"Yeah, that's right. Kill a defenseless man," Connie spoke up, wheeling her horse. "I'd expect no less from a coward like you. I bet all the coup you've counted has been on women, kids, and men who couldn't lift a finger to save their hides."

Minio reddened and stopped. "I kill many men who not tied, bitch. Many with bare hands. Everyone fear me." Raising the revolver, he took deliberate aim at her. "Maybe Snake not care if you missing ear."

Helpless on the ground, Fargo saw Minio smirk. He coiled his legs, about to throw himself at the renegade's legs, when the most remarkable thing happened. From out of nowhere a skinny arm and gnarled hand appeared, swinging from behind the Cheyenne, spearing a gleaming knife straight into Minio's throat.

The renegade recoiled and looked down at himself in amazement. He gawked at the hand holding the knife hilt and blurted, "What—?" Any other words he was going to say were stifled by the red gusher that spurted out of his mouth and sprayed from the wound in his neck. The hand tore the knife out, then plunged the blade in again, only lower. Minio sputtered, flung the revolver down, and grabbed at the skinny arm. Puffing and spitting blood, he tried to tear the knife out, but the skinny arm was as unyielding as solid rock. Minio's strength drained from him with incredible rapidity. His legs sagged. He wailed once, a strident screech that wavered on the wind, then pitched forward onto his face, convulsed, and was still.

Fargo barely noticed. He was staring, astounded, at the smiling Shoshoni holding the bloody knife. "You!" he exclaimed. "Where did you come from?"

Beaver Tail sighed and bent over to wipe his knife clean on Minio's leggings. "How can you ask such a stupid question?"

"Do you know this Indian?" Connie asked.

"He's a friend," Fargo said.

"And you are lucky I am," Beaver Tail declared, straightening. "If not, I would have left you and gone back to my people after you hurt my feelings." He walked up to Fargo. "But a true warrior forgives those of his friends who have no manners. It is not always their fault. Especially with white men, who are dead inside to the ways of the spirit."

Connie slid off her horse. "What is this old man talking about?"

"Half the time I don't think *he* knows," Fargo said, sitting up and extending his arms toward the Shoshoni. "Here. Cut me loose."

"Why should I when you have just insulted me again?" Beaver Tail asked stiffly.

"I'm sorry," Fargo snapped, glancing to the north. The dust cloud was gone. Snake and his men must be in the tract of forest bordering the valley.

"You do not sound sincere."

Fargo angrily swung his arms back and forth. "Damn it! Get this rope off me unless you figure you can whip Snake Haddock and his men all by yourself!"

"They are coming?"

"They'll be here in a minute."

"You should have said so sooner," Beaver Tail said, applying his knife to the rope. "Not that I am worried about myself. I can always turn invisible." The strands parted and the rope fell.

"Invisible?" Connie said.

"Later," Fargo said, retrieving his Colt. He checked the cylinder, then jammed the revolver into his holster. "Both of you mount and ride." Taking two bounds, he vaulted onto the Ovaro and whipped the Sharps out. Connie and Beaver Tail had not moved. "Are the two of you hard of hearing? Get the hell out of here before Snake shows up."

"It no longer matters if we leave or not," Beaver Tail said, pointing.

Fargo looked, knowing what he would see—five riders galloping down the valley toward them, five seasoned killers who were out for one thing, blood.

15

"Lose yourselves in the trees," Fargo advised Constance Jennings and the Shoshoni. Then, the Sharps resting across his thighs, he rode to meet the outlaws. They fanned out at a gesture from Snake Haddock, forming a line, spaced at five-yard intervals with Snake in the center. Fargo cocked his rifle.

At three hundred yards the outlaws slowed to a walk, each man pulling his rifle out. They totally ignored Connie and Beaver Tail. The Trailsman was the one they wanted, and their collective attention was fixed exclusively on him.

Fargo mentally gauged the distance, the wind, the slight elevation increase from one end of the valley to the other. Everything that might have a bearing on the accuracy of his shots was considered and noted. When the time came, he would be ready.

Snake Haddock drew within one hundred yards, then halted. His men did the same. Cupping a hand to his mouth, Snake shouted. "You've caused me a heap of grief, mister! Here's where I return the favor."

Raising the Sharps so that the stock rested on his right leg, Fargo made no reply. Given Haddock's temperament, not answering was sure to get the killer's goat. And it did.

"Cat got your tongue, bastard?" Snake said angrily.

Still Fargo said nothing.

One of the outlaws, Porter, said something to Haddock, who rose in the stirrups and gazed past Fargo. "Is that Minio I see lying there?"

Fargo smiled, a broad smile so they could all plainly see, and nodded. "Your mad dog has been cured of his rabies."

"That's a shame," Snake said, lowering onto his saddle. "Him and me went back a ways. This just gives me one more reason to do what I should have done the moment I laid eyes on you." He glanced at his men, then nodded.

Whooping and hollering, the outlaws charged and opened fire.

Fargo had the Sharps to his shoulder before his enemies spurred their mounts. He sighted on Snake Haddock first. No matter what else happened, he was going to get Snake. Should the outlaws slay him, he would at least have the pleasure of knowing he took one of the worst butchers on the frontier with him. His shot thundered just as Snake's horse surged into motion, and Haddock threw up his arms and toppled.

He reloaded swiftly, keenly aware of the bullets whizzing past. The outlaws all missed their first rushed volley. Firing a rifle from the back of a moving horse was never easy. It took an exceptional marksman to score hits with any consistency, and the outlaws were so eager to drop him that they weren't taking the time to aim as they should.

Fargo did not make the same mistake. He took a bead on a second man, who turned out to be Porter, and fired at the same instant Porter did. The outlaw's shot clipped his hat. His shot hit dead center, the slug boring through Porter's chest and slamming the man from his horse. Porter wound up in a disjointed heap on the ground.

Now Fargo spurred the Ovaro into a gallop, angling to the right, making himself a harder target to hit. He inserted a fresh round, snapped the Sharps up, and fired at an outlaw in the act of reloading. The man clutched at his head, screamed, then fell.

Only two hard cases remained, but they were both game. They swept toward Skye from the left, squeezing off shots as fast as they could, one of them standing in the stirrups.

Fargo turned and charged them head-on. They were fifty yards off and closing swiftly. Odds were that one of them would nail him unless he did the unexpected. With that in mind, he shoved the Sharps into the scabbard and bent low over the stallion's neck. Bullets buzzed past. He drew the Colt, then hooked his left elbow over the

Ovaro's neck and pressed his body against its side, riding Indian fashion, his right leg dangling, his left looped over the saddle.

Something smacked his left boot heel. The outlaws were shooting at the only part of him still visible, knowing if they damaged his left leg he would lose his purchase and fall. Little did they realize he intended to let go anyway. They expected him to sit up at the last moment and cut loose, and they would be ready for him. So to catch them off guard, he did the opposite.

Fargo waited until he glimpsed one of the outlaws forty feet off, bearing down on his side of the stallion for a better shot. Then he shoved off, landed hard in the grass on his right shoulder, and rolled three times before coming up on one knee with the Colt at waist height and his thumb on the hammer. The outlaw swung his rifle to compensate but he was too slow. Fargo fired twice and the man twisted, grabbed his chest, and tumbled.

Spinning, Fargo saw the last outlaw, whose rifle was empty, frantically clawing at a hip gun. Fargo's Colt boomed. A red hole blossomed above the man's right eye, and down he went. The outlaw's horse kept on running. Two of the other mounts were also galloping off. The dependable Ovaro, however, had stopped, just as Fargo had trained it to do.

After the thunder of the guns, the relative quiet seemed unnatural. Fargo's ears were ringing. He slowly stood and began removing the spent cartridges from his revolver. Behind him someone yelled, and he turned to see both Connie and Beaver Tail waving their arms and pointing at something farther up the valley.

One look sent a ripple of rage down his spine. Snake Haddock wasn't dead! The outlaw had climbed back on his horse and was making for the forest! He ran to the stallion and swung up. Haddock, doubled over and swaying, perhaps mortally wounded, was nonetheless close enough to the pines to be among them in seconds.

Fargo reached for the Sharps, realized he could not possibly get off a shot before the outlaw got to cover, and promptly gave chase. There was no way he would let Haddock escape. If he had to track the killer clear into Canada, so be it.

He saw Snake look back, then ride into the trees. If

the outlaw was smart, Fargo reasoned, Haddock would stop behind a pine and wait in ambush for him to appear. But Fargo wasn't about to do the obvious. Instead of entering the forest at the exact same point Snake did, he rode farther north, inserting new bullets into the Colt before he got to the tree line.

Holding the stallion to a walk, Fargo slipped into the woods. He stopped to scan the trees to the south but saw no sign of Snake. Was he wrong? Had the outlaw kept going? Fargo cautiously moved toward the spot he had last seen the killer, pausing often to look and listen. He came on fresh tracks, heading northeast, and cursed himself for being a fool for trying to outthink Haddock when all he really had to do was outride the son of a bitch.

Fargo stuck to the tracks, moving rapidly, noting drops of blood here and there that convinced him Snake was badly wounded. The trail led to a hill. At the base, Fargo halted, concerned Snake was lying for him on top. He could swing to either side and go up the slope from a different direction, but he'd already wasted valuable time trying to outsmart Haddock once and wasn't about to do so again.

He took the hill at a gallop, the stallion's powerful hoofs sending clods of dirt flying in their wake. At the crest he saw where Snake had stopped to check the back trail. Shielding the sun from his eyes with his left hand, he scoured the country ahead but saw nothing move.

From the hill the trail took him into more forest, along a winding valley, and near a mountain dotted with clusters of aspen. He glanced at the snowy crest and watched a bald eagle soar above it. His attention was diverted for only a few seconds, but when he looked at the ground again the tracks had vanished. Reining up, he shifted and stared at the earth behind him. Haddock had changed direction. The hoof prints now headed toward the mountain.

Fargo turned, and as he did the ground to the right of the Ovaro erupted in a geyser of dirt, and he heard the sharp report of a rifle. A flick of the reins and a jab of his heels galvanized the stallion into a race for the vegetation at the bottom of the facing slope. The rifle cracked again, but he had cut to the right. A zigzag pattern brought him to temporary safety among fir trees.

Jumping down, Fargo put the Colt in his holster and grabbed the Sharps. He worked the trigger guard and stuck in a cartridge. Then he climbed, going from tree to tree and boulder to boulder, never taking his eyes off the slope above him. Somewhere up there was one of the worst killers west of the Mississippi, and come what may only one of them would leave that mountain alive.

A slug nearly took his head off as he peeked around a boulder. Stone chips stung his cheek, and he threw himself backward and crouched, his pulse racing. Flattening, he snaked his way through heavy brush for a dozen yards, then he rose and resumed climbing.

He was almost to some aspen when a shot knocked his hat off. Taking a running dive, he came down on his elbows and knees between two slender trunks. Haddock was putting up a good fight. Each shot came closer than the last. If he wasn't more careful, Snake would add his name to the long list of those who had opposed the outlaw and paid for their folly with their lives.

Fargo glided through the aspens until he reached a clearing. Skirting it, he scaled a steep incline and found himself among waist-high boulders. He slid to a spot affording a choice view of the upper slope and went no farther.

The minutes dragged by. He studied every square foot of the mountain within his line of vision and saw nothing. The gunshots had driven all the wildlife into hiding, and not even a single chipmunk showed its little face. The eagle, too, was gone.

Fargo rested his chin in his hand and debated whether to keep going. If his patience was equal to the task, sooner or later he would spot Haddock. No sooner did the thought cross his mind than he detected movement on the top of a rock overhang eighty yards away. He froze, recognizing the outline of Haddock's head and shoulders.

Snake was searching for *him*.

Putting both hands down, he gripped the rifle and inched backward until he was behind a boulder. Then he eased onto his knees, tucked the Sharps to his shoulder, and rose high enough to see the overhang. Snake was still there, still scouring the slope. He slowly extended the barrel. Taking aim, he double-checked the sight before he cocked the hammer and set the trigger.

The outlaw suddenly looked right at him.

It was one of those rare moments when time stood still, when the simplest of acts took an eternity to complete, when everything that transpired became indelibly branded on the brain.

Fargo swore he saw Haddock's mouth fall open at the very instant he squeezed the trigger. The top of Snake's head blew off, yet somehow Snake got to one knee and tried to bring his rifle to bear. Fargo saw the outlaw lean forward, saw Snake's hand grab at thin air, and then Haddock slumped and plunged over the rim, bouncing off a boulder on the way down. Even at that distance Fargo heard the sickening thud when the body hit.

"I don't mind if he tags along with us," Connie said, bestowing a smile on Fargo that would have melted butter. "He's a sweet old man."

Fargo looked at Beaver Tail and grumbled, "I thought you were in a hurry to get back to your people."

"Not anymore," the Shoshoni replied. "It has been many winters since I last visited one of your strange villages made of wood and stone. I would like to do it one more time before I pass on to the spirit world, just to see if white men are still as crazy as I remember them."

Connie giggled. "Isn't he adorable?" She looked at Fargo. "Please let him come. It will be wonderful to have the extra company."

"If you say so," Fargo said, riding eastward. He had returned to the valley after verifying Snake Haddock was indeed dead to find Connie and the warrior joking and laughing together, the best of friends. First the Ovaro, now her. What was it about the old brave, anyway?

"You should be grateful to have me ride with you, Trailsman," Beaver Tail declared. "I can help when trouble comes, and it will come because you are the kind of man who brings trouble on himself just by breathing. I have known warriors like you. They see a bear far off, and it goes out of its way to attack them."

"We can get by quite well without you," Fargo said.

"You think so? Who was it who started a fire at the

entrance to the ravine so you could find it that much faster in the dark?"

"That was you?"

"Yes. Then I climbed on top of the ravine and tried to stop the bad men from getting through. But in the dark I could not see what to shoot."

Fargo yanked on the reins and turned. "You dunderhead!" he exploded. "That was us you shot at! We're lucky we're still alive."

"It was you?" Beaver Tail said sheepishly.

Connie wagged a finger at Fargo. "Don't be so hard on him. He was only doing what he thought was right. And none of us were hit."

"With friends like him . . ." Fargo muttered and left the statement unfinished. He shook his head in exasperation, then continued eastward.

"Maybe, if you treat Beaver Tail real nice, he'll show you what he's promised to show me," Connie said, sounding excited at the prospect.

"Which is?"

"Don't you know? Didn't you see how he killed that terrible renegade?"

"He sneeked up through the grass behind Minio and stabbed him."

"You've got it all wrong," Connie said. She nodded at the Shoshoni. "Tell him. He'll be amazed."

"I told him days ago and he did not believe me," Beaver Tail said, moving his horse close to hers and giving her arm a friendly pat. "Forget about him. He is not one for good manners." His forehead knit. "Do you remember what we were talking about when he came back? I think I do. It was the very first time I became invisible. I had only been in this world fifteen winters when I decided to go on a vision quest . . ."

Skye Fargo shut out the drone of the old man's voice, sighed, and gazed skyward. It was going to a long ride to the nearest settlement. A long, long ride.

LOOKING FORWARD!

**The following is the opening
section from the next novel in the exciting
Trailsman series from Signet:**

THE TRAILSMAN #136
TEXAS TRIGGERS

*Texas, 1860 . . .
on the edge of the Circle T Ranch,
a town called Deadwood, where broken men
lived or died by their trigger fingers
and a man's word was the only law. . . .*

A lonely sound. The goddamn loneliest sound in the world, he thought. The rhythmic creak of rope against the branch of the cottonwood tree carried faintly on the dry wind.

The pinto under him heard it too and shifted nervously, nostrils flaring. The horse shook its head and nickered low. The smell of blood always made it shy like that, he thought, narrowing his lake blue eyes.

Skye Fargo turned his gaze from the solitary tree and surveyed the gray chaparral which spread out around him in all directions. The thickets were pale green in places, beginning to bud in the early spring warmth. The land was broad and seemingly endless, crinkling off to the south into a gulch and probably a river, he thought, noting the darker band of low land. Ahead he saw short hills. The sun blazed overhead in the pale blue sky which faded to white at the distant horizon. There was no one in sight. Whoever had done it, had come and gone without waiting to see if the job was finished.

Excerpt from TEXAS TRIGGERS

Frontier justice was swift, he thought, as he put his spur to the Ovaro and galloped down the long slope toward the four men swinging from the cottonwood. Swift and sometimes dead wrong.

One of the men was still kicking, as if running from death. He dangled above the ground, his legs pumping in a hopeless struggle for breath as the knotted rope slowly strangled him. A hanged man was lucky if his neck broke immediately, Fargo thought, looking at the three still bodies hanging heavily from the tree. As he galloped nearer, he saw that the four had been shot, too. Blood darkened the front of their shirts. That was the scent the wind had carried to the Ovaro's sensitive nostrils. Fargo arrived just as the man's battle ended. The flailing legs suddenly lost power, twitched once, and were still.

Fargo sat on his pinto regarding the four men hanging before him, heads bent toward their shoulders, faces dark, hands tied behind their backs. The ropes groaned as the wind caught the bodies and swung them back and forth, back and forth. A hawk wheeled high overhead. The vultures would arrive soon.

He wondered who the men were. Horse thieves, murderers, bandits, maybe. But as he studied the men's clothing, he doubted it. They looked like ordinary cowpunchers, with their weather-stained chaps, rope-hardened hands, and wide brimmed hats. And they were just boys, younger than twenty, he guessed. One was tow-headed, one carrot-topped and two dark, maybe Mexican. Now, why would four young punchers get hanged in the middle of nowhere in Texas? Maybe they were part of a gang of rustlers.

It would be prudent to find out who they were, Fargo thought. If he could. He didn't know this part of southern Texas, but if somebody was out on a hanging spree, it would be a good idea to find out as much as possible.

Fargo drew his Colt and fired in rapid succession at the four ropes. The bodies fell, one by one, heavily onto the hard-packed dry earth. Fargo dismounted.

The redhead had nothing in his pockets but a well-fingered tintype of a saloon girl with one leg on a chair

Excerpt from TEXAS TRIGGERS

and her garters showing. Fargo replaced it in the boy's pocket.

One of the Mexican boys was lying on his side and, as Fargo turned the body faceup, the boy groaned faintly. Fargo loosened the rope around his neck, finding it was high around his ear, which had saved the boy from strangulation. But the bullet wound in his chest had hit just below the breastbone. Blood was flowing fast. He wouldn't last long no matter what, Fargo realized, and there was every possibility he shouldn't. For all he knew, the boy was a thief and was hanged justly. But somehow he found himself doubting it.

The boy's lids fluttered open, and the eyes, dark and soft brown, focused slowly on Fargo's face. The boy's lips moved slightly. He was trying to talk. Well, at least that would tell him something, Fargo thought.

Fargo fetched his canteen and splashed a few drops of water on the boy's lips. He could see the struggle on the boy's face as he tried to form words but failed. The sun beat down and Fargo felt the sweat drip from under his hat. He moved so that he shaded the boy from the sun's glare. After a moment, the boy tried again and the words came slowly.

"Take . . . message to . . . *Il Patrone*," the boy said in a heavy accent. Fargo nodded encouragement. "Please . . . take message or many more . . . many more will die." The boy paused and swallowed dry. Fargo splashed a little more water on his lips. A drink would only choke the boy now, and it wouldn't save his life. The boy's eyes shone gratitude for the water. "Please, promise," he muttered. "Promise . . ." The boy paused expectantly, his eyes begging Fargo for a reply.

"Promise," Fargo repeated, before he knew what he was doing. Relief washed over the boy's face.

"Promise" the boy repeated in his thick accent. "Tell *Il Patrone*. Only *Il Patrone* and no one else. No other person." He paused with the effort. "Tell *Il Patrone* that . . ." the voice weakened to barely a whisper. ". . . that team works for the sheriff. Team is against *Il Patrone* now." Fargo puzzled over the words, not sure if he had heard right.

Excerpt from TEXAS TRIGGERS

"The team works for the sheriff?" Fargo repeated. "The team is against *Il Patrone*?"

The boy's gaze clouded with frustration, and he looked as if he might speak again, but his eyes suddenly went dull and the mouth sagged open. Fargo eased the boy to the ground and went through his pockets.

Fargo found only knives, bits of jerky, and the one photograph on them—nothing that would shed light on who they were and why they were hanged. He laid the bodies out side by side and considered burying them. If they were thieves, they should be left to the vultures. But if they were innocent, they deserved a burial. Since he didn't know, he decided to leave them as they were. He remounted the pinto and rode west again in the direction he'd been heading, thinking about the boy's last words.

Fargo had been looking forward to a leisurely trip across Texas to New Orleans, where he'd been planning a long overdue month of relaxation. The image of a dark-haired Creole woman with a slender waist floated up before him, and for a moment he felt the pull of her. He should forget the hanging incident and ride on.

But Fargo had given his promise. The boy had died believing that the stranger who leaned over him would deliver his message to *Il Patrone*. Whoever the hell that was. And, according to the kid, the team was on the side of the sheriff. If he delivered the message, would he be helping the wrong side, Fargo wondered.

The boy's voice still echoed in his ears, "Take message or many more die." The question was, if he found *Il Patrone* and delivered the boy's message, would it save the lives of thieves? Or of innocent people?

A mile farther, Skye spotted a saddled horse grazing alone. He galloped over, prepared to rope it. But it did not move at his approach. He slowed, leaned out from his pinto and caught up the reins of the docile chestnut, pulling her alongside.

The saddle was spattered with blood, a dark stain on the leather-covered horn and the front of the seat. It was nearly new, the leather still pale honey and, except for the blood, unstained. Fargo noted the heads of longhorn

Excerpt from TEXAS TRIGGERS

steers tooled on the fenders which hung down on either side. He examined the stamp of the Kansas City maker on the corner of the skirt. His eye was caught by a brand on the chestnut's haunch—T enclosed by an O. The Circle T, Fargo thought to himself, since brands were always read from the outside in.

He'd heard of the Circle T Ranch, reputed to be the biggest spread in Texas. But its size was all he knew about it. No doubt the chestnut had belonged to one of the four dead boys. So they had come from the Circle T.

Unless they had stolen the mount. But in that case, whoever hanged them would have caught the horse and taken it back to the ranch. None of it made sense. Maybe he would meet someone who could enlighten him, he thought as he tied the horse behind him and rode on.

"Deadwood, Texas," the tilted sign read. "Leave your gun in your holster. Population . . ." Beneath the last line were several figures. One hundred seventy-three had been scratched out as had one hundred forty-nine and several more numbers. The final figure written was eighty-four but someone had marked through that as well and not bothered to add another.

A well stood in the middle of the wide dusty street or rather in the middle of the space between the buildings, since there were hardly enough of them to define a street. A few board shacks were scattered along one side. An imposing gallows of weathered gray board crooked a tall finger against the sky. From it swung two empty nooses. A moving figure caught Fargo's eye and he reined in.

A man was dragging a body by the feet and disappeared between two of the shacks. At the other end of the street, Fargo saw a second body lying in the dust. Even at a distance, Fargo's keen eyesight could make out the silver pistol still in the hand of the outflung arm, the natty clothing of the professional gunslinger, and the blood pooling darkly to one side of the body. All was silent, still.

A big mud-brick building with barred windows and a pointed tin roof sported a sign reading "County Bank,

Excerpt from TEXAS TRIGGERS

All Deposits Welcome." Across the way was a corral, stable, and a few more board shacks. Fargo heard a sound and moved forward. In a side yard, a man was hammering together a coffin and didn't look up as Fargo clopped down the street. Otherwise there was no one in sight.

A tall false-fronted building with batwing doors had a few horses tethered outside. Fargo headed for it, wondering who had been in the shoot-out. Maybe someone in the saloon would know who *Il Patrone* was. And what the hangings were all about.

Fargo pushed inside the doors, entering the murky room. As his eyes adjusted to the dimness, he heard the sound of sudden movement, of men pushing their chairs away from the tables and of guns being cocked. He paused and surveyed the saloon, squinting in the gloom. A dozen men had hunkered down around the room, all with their attention on him. Half had ducked behind tables, and several had their pistols drawn and cocked.

"Expecting somebody?" Fargo said with a grin. He slowly moved his hands out from his hips to show he had no intention of drawing. Nobody moved.

"What d'ye want, stranger?" a thick voice asked. Fargo located the speaker, a black-bearded man with a pot belly standing by the bar. He held an Allen and Thurber Dragoon in front of him, a model from the gold rush days. They weren't accurate, but the old '49ers could make a nasty hole at close range, Fargo thought, looking down the broad barrel.

"Passing through. Just stopped for a friendly drink," Fargo answered, his voice not at all friendly. Some welcome to Deadwood, he thought.

Fargo raised his hands slightly, further from his Colt. His tall muscular frame was tense, hearing alert, ready to draw at any sudden motion from the men. After a long moment, the man at the bar relaxed and holstered his pistol. The rest of the men did as well, returning to their chairs.

"Never can be too sure," the man mumbled. Fargo walked into the saloon, or what passed for one in Deadwood, Texas, and joined the black-bearded man at the

Excerpt from TEXAS TRIGGERS

bar. The man didn't look at him, and Fargo turned to survey the room.

Five rickety tables and a bunch of mismatched chairs filled the small dark chamber. The men in dusty clothes and weather-beaten hats hunched over card games. One wall was covered, floor to ceiling, with sun-bleached skulls—buffalo, antelope, armadillo, cougar, badger, even a couple of human ones, all jumbled together.

As Fargo turned back, a skinny bartender poked his head above the counter, behind which he'd been hiding.

"Help you?" he asked, eyes darting nervously.

"What's the local brew?" Fargo asked.

"Redeye."

"Some of that," Fargo said. He watched as the man poured two fingers into a shot glass and slid it across the bar. Just as Fargo raised it to his mouth, a second figure appeared from behind the counter.

The woman was plump in all the right places, dark-eyed and dark-haired, probably from across the border, he thought. She pulled her shawl close about her and caught his eye. He smiled encouragingly. She looked away, and he tipped up the glass.

"Had a shoot-out?" Fargo asked the black-bearded man standing next to him.

After a minute the man grunted assent.

"Who was it?" Fargo asked, idly rolling the empty glass between his fingers.

The man shrugged. Another moment passed. The bartender noticed Fargo's glass was empty and refilled it.

"You got a helluva lot of questions, stranger," the man muttered. It was Fargo's turn to shrug and he did.

"We get a lot of gunslingers coming through," the man added. "Can't keep track of 'em all."

"Where's the sheriff?" Fargo asked.

The man shrugged again.

"Out," he finally said. Another minute passed, and Fargo assumed the conversation was over.

"Riding around," the man added at last.

If he expected answers from this man, he'd be waiting forever, Fargo realized. He turned his attention toward the girl.

Excerpt from TEXAS TRIGGERS

"Well?" the bartender whispered, nudging her. "Get over there." She flicked the bartender an angry look and came around the bar, sidling up next to Fargo, who drank the second glass down.

Redeye was well named, Fargo thought, his eyes watering slightly from the fire of the brew. A few of the men left the bar. Others were engrossed in serious card playing and drinking. The black-bearded man joined one of the games. Fargo glanced down at the woman at his elbow.

"My name is Lucia," she said, almost in a whisper. Her Spanish accent was unmistakable. "What's yours?"

"Skye Fargo," he answered with a nod.

"Nice name," she said, blinking her long dark lashes. Her eyes glanced at the empty glass. "Another?"

Before he answered or even nodded, the bartender reached for the shot glass and refilled it hastily. So that was the game, Fargo thought, his eyes lingering on her low neckline. She'd get the customers drunk. Then take them up the back stairs. Or rob them. Or worse. He'd seen the game before. Fargo wrapped his large fist around the shot glass, but kept it on the countertop.

"Where're you from?" he asked. Her dark brows shot up in surprise.

"Me? From?" Lucia looked surprised to be asked a question. "Piedritas," she answered. "Across the border." The bartender had begun to dry glasses, humming to himself, but clearly listening to every word.

"What are you doing up here?" Fargo asked, still not taking a drink. She was damn pretty. And very young. Too much of both to be stuck in this dead-end town. Lucia smiled up at him, responding to his interest.

"I was looking for my sister. And this is as far as I got when I ran out of money. My sister's name is Angelina." He smiled at her, nodding. Then her words came out in a rush, as if they'd been dammed up for a long time and had needed release. "Maybe you have seen her. She looks like me, Angelina. But she is older—" The bartender, his back turned to them, rapped a glass on the bar, a clear signal she wasn't doing her job. Lucia looked flustered for an instant.

Excerpt from TEXAS TRIGGERS

"But . . . but what about you?" she asked, looking up and blinking her eyes at him again. Poor kid, he thought. She ran out of money in Deadwood, Texas. What luck. He smiled at her but didn't answer. "Please, drink." She gestured toward the redeye.

"I'll switch to beer," Fargo said. He wanted to keep his wits about him. But it would be pleasant to have some female company for a couple of hours. And maybe he could find out something from her, easier than from the laconic men. He tossed coins down on the counter and took up the two beers the bartender poured, leaving the shot of redeye on the bar.

"Let's get over here," Fargo said, leading her to a just-vacated table under a sun-bleached buffalo skull with each socket the size of two fists. As he settled in, he noticed the bartender pick up the abandoned shot glass, shrug, and carefully pour the redeye back into the bottle.

"So, what's this about your sister?" he asked, sliding her one of the beers. She took it and smiled.

"I heard she headed this direction . . . but, you don't want to hear my troubles," she added, embarrassed.

"Then, tell me about the shoot-out," he said, nodding toward the street. He would start with the obvious questions and see if he could get a sense of the place. Maybe she'd know something, maybe she wouldn't.

"Oh that," she said shrugging as the man at the bar had. "There's a shoot-out every day, it seems."

"And the sheriff doesn't do anything about it?"

"Him!" She spit on the floor before she could stop herself, then looked down. "He's hardly ever in town anyway. There are big troubles on the ranch south of here."

"What kind of trouble?"

"Rustlers. It's the Spill brothers and their gang."

"I've heard of them," Fargo said. "They've been rustling for a long time."

"Yes," Lucia said, taking a swallow of the beer. "We know them in Mexico, too. Anyway, the Spill brothers came through Deadwood a while back. The sheriff caught them and locked them up. But, the night before he was

Excerpt from TEXAS TRIGGERS

going to hang them, they escaped. They're out there somewhere, stealing longhorns from the big ranch."

"The Circle T?"

"Yes, that's the name."

"And the sheriff's gone to the ranch to help?"

"Not exactly. He and his posse have been patrolling the border of the Circle T," she said. Her eyes glittered as if she were happy to be telling him a secret. "There is something strange about that because everybody says he is not welcome on the ranch. The ranch hands don't like anybody to come onto the ranch. Especially the sheriff."

"How can they stop him?"

"The Circle T has . . . riders; they call them . . ."

"Line riders?" Fargo guessed.

"Yes, that is the word. Line riders. These men ride all around the ranch to keep people out."

"And the cattle in," Fargo said.

"I suppose," she said doubtfully. "But, they say if you go on the Circle T land, these riders will shoot you first. They keep to themselves on the Circle T."

"So, why is the sheriff helping them?"

Lucia grinned and pointed to a piece of paper tacked to one wall. Fargo rose and went to inspect it. On the wanted poster were the two faces of the Spill brothers crudely drawn. It read: "Wanted, Dead or Alive: Spill Bros. Jas. & Theo . . . $1,000 Reward for Both. $400 for One." He sat back down beside Lucia.

"That's a hefty reward."

"People say that the sheriff's mad as a hornet that the Spill brothers got away. They're impossible to catch," she said. "But I think the sheriff wants the money very much. Ever since they escaped, the sheriff's been out all the time trying to find them."

Fargo smiled at her and she smiled back, her round cheeks dimpling. His mind was in a whirl. Maybe the four kids had been from the Spill Brothers gang. But even as he thought this, he felt it was wrong. They just didn't look like rustlers. He'd try a more interesting question on her.

"Ever hear of *Il Patrone*?" he asked.

Excerpt from TEXAS TRIGGERS

"Il Patrone?" she repeated, her eyes thoughtful. "It means The Patron in your language." She thought a moment and then shook her head. "No, it does not mean anything to me. But it is a title of great honor in my country. Only great men are called *Il Patrone*."

Fargo nodded and took a swallow of beer.

"Any great men around here?" he said, looking furtively toward the dusty men playing cards. She giggled and then grew serious.

"Well, there is Mr. Owen Tate," she said.

"Who's that?" Fargo asked.

"He owns the Circle T," Lucia answered. "He is the most powerful man in Texas. Maybe in the whole country. But I hear he is a very bad man, very dangerous."

"Dangerous?" he repeated. "How so?"

"Well, I don't know," she said slowly. "That is what people say. I guess he is so powerful that, on his ranch, everyone does what he says. His word is the law."

"That could be dangerous," Fargo agreed, thinking of the four dead boys. "What does he look like?"

Lucia laughed.

"No one ever sees Mr. Owen Tate! Even his men do not come into Deadwood. They always stay on the ranch. I hear the Circle T is so big a man can ride for three days and hardly make it across."

Fargo nodded. He had heard that, too. The idea of all that land belonging to one man was staggering. Why, with enough men like Owen Tate, there wouldn't be any free room on the plains. He shook his head slowly at the thought and set his empty glass down on the table.

"I'll get us another round," Lucia said, rising. A rangy fellow entered the doors and approached the bar at the same moment she did. The man removed his hat and combed lanks of greasy hair back from his sweating face. Then he rubbed his hand down his shirt.

"Hot out," he grumbled to no one in particular.

Lucia stood waiting to get the beers. The man looked down at her, then reached over and put his hand on her rear. She stepped out of his reach.

"Whattsa matter?" he said to her. "Gimme a double shot," he added over his shoulder.

Excerpt from TEXAS TRIGGERS

The bartender left the beers and hastened to do his bidding. Meanwhile the man grabbed Lucia around the waist and drew her close. She struggled.

"Let me go," she said. "I am busy now. Later."

Fargo pushed his chair back noisily and slowly rose to his full height. The man looked up from Lucia, his eyes squinting as if taking Fargo's measure.

"The lady's with me at the moment," Fargo said.

One corner of the man's mouth twitched, then slowly raised in a half smile.

"I don't feel like waiting," the man said. He pulled her closer and grabbed one of her breasts with his free hand. "This little woman's gonna give me what I want when I want it."

She pushed him away firmly and turned again to the bar. The man grabbed her arm, hard, and pulled her back toward him.

"I think the lady should make up her own mind," Fargo said.

"Have it your way," the man said, pushing her roughly toward him. Lucia fell to the floor, and the man turned away toward the bar. Fargo stepped forward and gave her a hand up. He had just headed back toward the table when he heard the unmistakable soft whisper of a pistol drawn from a leather holster.

He pushed Lucia off to one side and dove in the opposite direction as the crack of the gunshot split the air where he had been standing. Fargo landed in the middle of a card game and rolled away instantly as the table collapsed under him. He came up on his feet, Colt in hand. All around him, men ducked for cover.

The man stood ten feet from him, pistol drawn, eyes narrowed to black slits. Fargo noted that he held his gun expertly, firm in the palm, low down by the hip. The man would be a good shot and had very nearly shot him in the back with no warning. Still, he was reluctant to gun a man down over bad manners.

"Where I come from, we don't shoot men in the back," Fargo said, his voice low.

"In Deadwood, we shoot 'em any way we can," the

Excerpt from TEXAS TRIGGERS

man answered. Fargo waited a moment, considering the situation.

"Walk out of here now, and we'll call it quits," Fargo said calmly, his finger firm on the trigger. The man looked at him for a long moment, and the corner of his mouth twitched again, very slightly, then curled up in a half smile.

"Sure," the man said. "Sure." He lowered his gun, and Fargo did likewise, both of them slowly holstering them as they kept their eyes locked on each other. But before the man had completely holstered his pistol, he drew again in a flash. Fargo was ready. He crouched to one side, pulled up his Colt and fired. The gun exploded; the shot caught the man in his chest, and he spun almost all the way around before he slumped onto the floor.

Fargo felt a hot burn along one shoulder as he tumbled onto the wooden planked floor. He rolled once and came to his feet, advancing on the fallen figure.

Fargo kicked the gun out of the man's hand as he lay, blank-faced, staring up at the pressed tin ceiling. The wound in his chest spurted blood that made a bright red pool beside the body. There was silence in the saloon.

"Goddamn," the bartender said, raising up on his toes to look over the counter at the dead man. "Goddamn," he repeated, his face ashen. "You are in real trouble, stranger. You just shot the sheriff's chief deputy. He's gonna be pissed. Real pissed."